The South Carolina
Lizard Man

The South Carolina Lizard Man

By
NANCY RHYNE

Illustrated by
MAURO MAGELLAN

PELICAN PUBLISHING COMPANY
Gretna 1992

Library of Congress Cataloging-in-Publication Data

Rhyne, Nancy, 1926-
The South Carolina lizard man / by Nancy Rhyne ; illustrated by Mauro Magellan.
p. cm.
Summary: In 1846, while exploring the swamp on their South Carolina rice plantation, fifteen-year-old twins Josh and Matt find a seven-foot-tall lizardlike creature that walks on its hind legs.
ISBN 0-88289-907-4
[1. Monsters—Fiction. 2. Swamps—Fiction. 3. Twins—Fiction. 4. Brothers—Fiction. 5. South Carolina—Fiction.] I. Magellan, Mauro, ill. II. Title.
PZ7.R3479So 1992
[Fic]—dc20 92-17289
CIP
AC

Manufactured in the United States of America
Published by Pelican Publishing Company, Inc.
1101 Monroe Street, Gretna, Louisiana 70053

For

Garry,
a skilled boatman
who knows every nautical mile
from
Key West to the Marquesas islands
and
believes in sea monsters

ACKNOWLEDGMENTS

The author would like to thank Bill Starr of *The State* and Rich Oppel of *The Charlotte Observer* for permission to quote from their newspapers.

PROLOGUE

In the summers of 1815, 1816, 1817, 1818, 1819, and 1820, an eighty-foot snakelike creature was seen frolicking off the coast of Massachusetts. Due to multiple reports of sightings of the monster to the New England Linnean Society, the length was agreed to. "I have often seen many whales at sea," said Amos Story, "but this animal was much swifter than any whale. He had the head of a serpent, rather larger than his body."

On April 10, 1977, a thirty-two-foot sea serpent with four giant flippers was caught in a fishnet pulled by a Japanese trawler. It looked for all the world like a plesiosaur, a prehistoric marine animal that lived over two hundred million years ago and had a small head, long neck, four paddlelike limbs, and a short tail.

In the summer of 1988, deep in Scape Ore Swamp, about four miles south of Bishopville, South Carolina, a scaly green creature about seven feet tall with red, glaring eyes was seen. It had no human features, but as it was about seven feet tall and stood on its hind legs, it was called "The South Carolina Lizard Man." It nearly chewed up Tom and Mary Waye's car, and *The Charlotte Observer* and *The State* gave daily updates on its spirited actions. Also on a daily basis, all major networks of national television kept America abreast of the creature's comings and goings.

The story that follows is based on the dread reign of The South Carolina Lizard Man of Scape Ore Swamp. As we look backward to its ancestors, we are introduced to an earlier Lizard Man, a monster of hideous conformation who lived in and around another world of shadows—Hell Hole Swamp, near Charleston.

1

JOSH AND MATT were walking in the woods that April afternoon, talking about going to college in England in the fall. Not that they wanted to go, and not that they felt they needed further education. The tutors that had been brought to the South Carolina plantation near Charleston and even nearer to hazardous and shadowy Hell Hole Swamp had taught the twin boys everything they probably would ever need to know when they became rice planters, and other things that they might never need, such as Greek and Latin. And music even. But those were the subjects young men studied in 1846, and Matt and Josh hadn't the remotest intention of disappointing their parents who had seen to it that they would be sent to England when they reached fifteen.

They had only four months left on the plantation, The Bond, before they would sail on a schooner that would be loaded with enough Carolina rice to pay for the journey. The three-masted sailing vessel, being a part of the properties of the wealthy Bondurants, was also named *The Bond*, but before the time came to board the vessel and ride down to Charleston and off to England, Josh and Matt Bondurant decided to have an adventure of their very own. Yes sirree. They'd never been allowed to explore Hell Hole Swamp, and they decided to take a close look.

* * *

It's not always summer in April in other parts of the country, but on the coast of South Carolina it is warm enough to go barefoot, and Josh and Matt wore no shoes as they meandered along a familiar road. Johnnycake Road led to a fork where two other roads went in opposite directions. One of the avenues was Ropemaker's Lane, named for an old man who made ropes there, and the other road was known as The Shadows. It was a dark and forbidding passage to Hell Hole Swamp, a horrible, slimy place on which the twins had never laid their eyes.

"So, Twin," Josh needled as they sauntered along. "Are you going to shine as a scholar at Cambridge?"

"We'll have to wait and see, Harebrain," Matt answered. Although the twins loved each other, there was a constant banter between them.

"Everyone knows you're the Bondurant brain and I'm the entertaining one," Josh said as he jumped up to grab a twig.

"So? How're you going to be entertaining at Cambridge?"

"You'll see. You can call me 'Josh, the Jokester.'"

"Yes. That's entertaining!"

"Think there'll be any ladies there?" Josh asked.

Matt shot his brother a quick glance and laughed. "What do you *think*? That England is filled only with men? That's folly."

"All right, Genius. What are English ladies like?"

"That's easy enough. They're like ladies everywhere. They have long hair and wear hoop skirts, and they're, uh, sort of pretty."

Josh, now chewing on the twig, said, "Do you plan to pick one out? As sort of special?"

Matt's voice became more calm and pleasant. "Probably."

"You'll find one with intellect, and you can write poetry to her," Josh said, giggling.

Matt playfully slapped his brother on the shoulder. "Cut it out, Scatterbrain, or I'll write poetry about you, and when it's published in the school publication you'll come home on the next vessel." It was true that Matt was the studious twin, but he could also be as frisky as a colt. "Race you to the Lydia Oak," he said suddenly.

"Put your feet to the sand," Josh responded, already breaking into a run.

Josh beat his brother to the phantomlike tree that grew differently from the others in the forest. Lightning from summer storms frequently chose that tree to strike, and although it towered high, it had many scars.

Josh slid to a stop and sat down under the tree, which stood at the fork in the road. Low-hanging, curving limbs were draped with Spanish moss, and Josh leaned back and lay on the ground, looking up through the twisted limbs. "Oh dear me, I'm out of breath," he said to himself.

"That little race do you in?" Matt asked, now coming to a halt.

Josh sat up. "You noticed who won the race."

Matt didn't answer the wisecrack, but gazed at the tree. "That Lydia Oak affects me every time I see it. I wonder if that story about Lydia is true anyway."

"Course it's true. You think all the tales about the plantation are fiction?"

"Well, that particular story is a savage affair," Matt answered.

"No matter. All the old tales have drama," Josh said, now serious.

Matt sat down by his brother, looked up through the tangled limbs to the sky, and thought about what had happened at the tree.

The story was told that a milliner from Charleston, a beautiful young woman named Lydia, came to The Bond on a visit. While there she decided to take for herself any of the heirloom jewelry she found to her liking, but when the theft was discovered, she tried to burn down the mansion and hide her crime. Fortunately, the fire was put out quickly, and the mansion was saved. But Lydia was hanged from that very tree, and from that day on it was called the Lydia Oak.

"I suppose the story is true," Matt said. "It is always

told the very same way and with great detail, even down to the style of the hats that Lydia brought with her from Charleston. But do you believe that Lydia actually comes back to this tree as a ghost?"

"Of course I believe it," Josh answered, then added, "I haven't actually seen a ghost, but I wouldn't want to be where I am now, under this tree, after dark."

Matt jumped up. "Then we'd better get on our way. Hell Hole Swamp isn't around the next curve, and there are about a million curves in The Shadows from what I've heard."

Josh got up, stood by his brother, and looked reflectively at the lonely lane. It was a frightening road, and some believed that phantoms walked there. Even some of the trees looked like ghosts, with limbs going in every direction and covered with moss. And the shadows. They were everywhere. "You'll see a ghost or worse if we dare to travel that path to Hell Hole Swamp."

"I thought that was the plan, Bonehead," Matt said, now clearly agitated.

"You still want to go through with it?"

"Of course. Don't you?'"

"Oh, I reckon so. But there must be a good reason why our parents never allowed us to come here."

Matt let out a hearty laugh. "Listen to my twin. You're almost fifteen and scared to walk a road on Father's plantation."

"I am *not* afraid," Josh said, wondering if Matt would dare tell anyone in England about his fear. He didn't believe that Matt would tease him in front of others, but one never knew for sure. And he didn't want Matt to have something to hold over his head when they reached their college in England. Josh planned to make friends there, friendships that would endure for his lifetime. He and Matt had no really close friends in South Carolina, as the plantations were large estates. They only saw other planter families when they visited, which was rare, or on Sundays, at Goose Creek Church.

"Well, I am not afraid in the least," Matt stated, although not quite truthfully. "But I think we should observe Hell Hole Swamp in sunlight, and be far away when screech owls cry and mad dogs howl."

"And ghosts, dreamlike, float up from their graves?" Josh asked.

"That's it. Are you with me?"

"I'm with you," Josh answered, studying his brother. They were the same height, and both had brown hair and blue eyes. Most people could not tell them apart. And they were both determined to go to Hell Hole Swamp.

But Josh didn't break into a run as he usually did when exploring plantation backwoods.

2

WHICH, OF COURSE, was ridiculous. Josh should have taken off in a dash, running wildly to disguise the queasiness in the pit of his stomach. Although the road was cleared, it was plain to see that the woods on either side were a jungle, and only the Lord knew just what species of wildlife lurked there. "How many trees can you identify?" Josh asked, in an effort to keep his mind occupied on something other than the surroundings.

"There's oak, and pine, and cypress."

"Don't forget laurel, magnolia, and holly," Josh added.

"And Spanish sword," Matt said, chatting a little more lightly and easily than usual to mask a nagging anxiety. Spanish sword was a sort of palm tree, with sharp fronds that looked like swords, and the daggers pointed toward the sky from nearly every part of the forest floor. Just then Matt's gaze fell on something in the ditch by the road. "What do you think that is?"

Josh squinted. "Some kind of animal. Possibly a raccoon."

"Why's it lying in the ditch?" Matt asked just before he ran to the ball of brown fur.

"I'll wager its mother abandoned it," Josh said.

"And you can be sure she didn't intend to. She was probably killed, or something."

Josh stooped down and lifted the furry animal, and remembered some abandoned animals he and Matt had raised to maturity. "I've had some raccoon friends before," he said to the little ball of fur. "Father has rescued several raccoons like you, and my brother and I played with them and took care of them." He turned the tiny face with the delicate nose toward his brother. "Meet my twin, Matt."

Matt patted the bushy, grayish-white tail, and the animal's beady eyes shined from patches of black fur that ringed them. Then Matt contemplated the jungle of gnarled trees that were entwined with vines as large as his father's arms, a place that was surely filled with terrors. "What're we going to do with him?"

Josh was now filled with the pleasure that comes from holding a tiny animal, and the animal, who seemed to sense that he was with a friend, settled down in the crook of Josh's arm. "We're going to take him home, of course," Josh said. "You don't think we'd leave him here to be eaten by a bear, do you?"

"He is your property, sire," Matt replied, "but we've got to hurry if we want to get to Hell Hole Swamp and back before darkness sets in."

"Say, raccoon," Josh said playfully. "Have you heard the story about Lydia, the ghost?"

"Don't be ridiculous," Matt protested. "Animals can't understand English."

"How do you know? Have you ever been an animal?" Josh asked without taking his eyes from the ball of fur in the crook of his arm.

"I don't know," Matt answered, gazing around at the ghoulish surroundings. "Mother says I'm a pig, when I don't use good manners at the table."

"Well then, you're an animal who understands English," Josh said, turning his attention and words back to the raccoon. "Everybody who has seen Lydia has testified that she wears a white dress, and sits on a limb of the Lydia Oak and dangles her feet."

"This place has an aspect of such dreary desolation it seems untouched by the foot of a human being," Matt said, bringing Josh back to the shadowy landscape. Shadows

of every shape and pattern were everywhere, and the grotesque trees seemed to have a certain brooding appearance that made them almost lifelike. While some of the limbs meandered just above ground, others had no embellishment such as leaves or moss and they pointed up, out, and down, like long, sharp fingers.

Now approaching a bend in the road, Matt and Josh journeyed on, not knowing what to expect next.

They walked around the bend, and there, stretched out before them, was surely the most gruesome swamp that existed in the entire world. In the center was a pool covered with green slime, and even the pool resembled an octopus, as the center mass flowed into ditches and inlets that curved like tentacles. Cypress roots jutted from all parts of the water, and low-growing limbs were draped with Spanish moss that hung to the pool's surface and floated on the slime. It was a dark, somber, brooding place, and the atmosphere was dank.

"Wow-ee!" Josh exclaimed, still holding on to the raccoon. "You see that log?"

"That's no log, but an alligator."

"No. Not that one. I mean that log with the cooters on it."

Matt looked in another direction and saw a log with so many turtles hanging on it that it was a wonder the log didn't sink. "How many turtles are clinging to that log?"

"I don't know. I'm not counting."

"Josh, see that bead on the water, coming toward us?"

"That black thing in the slime?"

"Yep. It looks like a bead, but it's a snake head."

"What kind of snake?" Josh stepped backward.

"A water snake, but it could be as deadly as a viper."

The snake turned in another direction, and Josh said, "I'd suggest that we go home, but since we're here, we should take a good look." As he took in the sight, his face was as rigid as stone. Just then he saw a soft, green, mossy area. "Boy, that moss looks cool."

Matt's eyes went to the velvety green area beside the trunk of a massive oak tree whose limbs circled just above the water. "That's moss, but it's different from Spanish moss. I'll try to remember to look up moss in Father's library and get the exact species."

"It's sure shiny," Josh answered, not even thinking about a wisecrack that would have come at any other time. "Think we can sit on it for a spell?"

"Don't sit anywhere at Hell Hole Swamp," Matt cautioned. "Remember this place has breathing, living enemies everywhere, and they are so attuned to their surroundings that we cannot recognize them. If we let down our guard, we could be devoured."

"Oh, I don't know about that," Josh said, patting the head of the raccoon.

"Well, just look over your head."

Josh looked up just in time to see a snake slithering near his face.

3

"MOVE, JOSH! MOVE!"

Josh stumbled backward and fell, but he held on to the raccoon. Lying on his back and looking at the glimpses of sky beyond the network of tree limbs, a strange pensiveness came over him. Even in such creepy surroundings, a sort of dreaminess enveloped his brain, and he thought of the delights and dangers that he would miss when he went to England. Hell Hole Swamp filled him with a fascination that he would forever remember, but the plantation had offered so many opportunities for adventure, and no portion of the vast tract of land was more mysterious and beautiful than the salt marshes.

Tidewater flowed through the cordgrass in the marshes, and in the sunlight the waterways looked like bright blue ribbons in the grasses. The salt marshes were half-land, half-water, and during daylight they were like a watercolor painting. But at night, when wildlife ventured to the water's edge, and sea creatures pulled themselves from the murky brine, it could be a dangerous place to visit, unless one was in a boat. Many times Josh and Matt had gone into the marsh in a vessel, always with their father present, and those times were among the ones that he would dream of most when he was far away in England.

Once, Mr. Bondurant took his twins into the marsh by boat in the middle of the night. Matt and Josh held lighted torches as they sat behind their father, who rowed the cypress dugout canoe. Now and then Mr. Bondurant stopped the boat, and as it rocked gently, the boys held the torches near the water and quietly watched as crabs, conchs, and other water animals slowly made their way along the floor of the lagoon. The spectacle was forever changing and as one creature moved out of the circle of light from the torch another came along. The twins gave their closest attention to the panorama taking place before their eyes. As Josh thought back on such sweet and haunting memories, Matt startled him out of the reverie.

"Hey, Twin. Don't you think you'd better come out of your daydreaming?"

"That moss is so bright I'll bet it glows in the dark like a candle," Josh said, making an effort to reestablish the conversation.

"Oh, you're being amusing! That moss wouldn't glow in the dark." But as Matt looked closely, he wasn't so sure. "It *is* the most brilliant color of green that I have ever seen."

"Yes. And it's shiny," Josh added. "It's almost like wet skin, don't you think, Matt?"

"Yes, but that's just moisture that's gathered on the tufts. It looks like a good, soft place to rest, but I don't think resting is on our schedule when we're at this place. I'd hate to be caught here in the dark when the breeze starts to sigh."

"We'd better get home," Josh said. "Since the day we were born, this place has been off limits to us."

Matt turned. "We've finally seen Hell Hole Swamp, and for me, I don't care if I ever see it again. Let's go."

Josh started to turn around but stopped.

"What's wrong?" Matt asked.

Josh tilted his head. "Do you feel like somebody is watching us?"

"Watching us?"

"That's what I said, Brain." Josh was becoming nervous and fast losing his patience.

"I don't know," Matt said. "There is sort of a presence

here. I *do* feel something, but I can't say just what it is."

Josh's eyes were still on the moss, wet and shiny. "That moss couldn't be watching us."

"Maybe we're just imagining things," Matt said. "There're so many ghastly stories about this place, like that old woman who walks at midnight with her lamp."

"Yes. She went out with her lamp in the lull of a hurricane, and the river was rising and she was drowned. But she wouldn't be watching us. She only comes at night, they say."

"It's like, uh, like something or someone's eyes are boring into me," Matt observed.

"Exactly. You've described the feeling perfectly, but where are the eyes? Whose eyes are they?" Josh stood rigidly. "It couldn't be that moss. That's absurd." And just then something about the moss changed, and the grain or finish of the surface was more of a matte. What had originally appeared wet and shiny had become a dull expanse. "Matt?"

"What?"

"You know how the rice fields look in summer, when the sun shines on them and gives them a shiny green look, and then the wind ruffles them and they change, and as far as the eye can see the fields have a different look?"

"Sure. Everybody's noticed that. The rice fields in summer look like a sea of green, and then the wind blows the plants in a different direction, and the color changes slightly."

"Well, there is no wind here, but that moss just changed color," Josh said.

"What are you saying, Chucklehead?"

"Call me Chucklehead if you like, but you'd better get serious. That moss just moved," Josh explained.

"Josh—*please*! Moss can't move."

"You are right, Matt. Moss can't move. That green stuff we've been gazing at isn't moss. It's alive."

"You're being foolish, Josh. It's mad to think the moss

is alive," Matt answered, but just then there was a certain hush, a stillness to the swamp that had not been there before. No frog or cricket made a sound. No leaf moved and the Spanish moss hanging from the trees was perfectly still. "Something *is* strange," Matt agreed. Then he added, "I believe the moss *is* moving."

The swamp was choked with overhanging growth, but in the dimness of the scene both Matt and Josh sensed a movement, and they felt they were being scrutinized by some dark, forbidding eyes. Was it an omen, a sign that something was about to happen?

"Matt, do you feel like you cannot move?"

"I feel like my feet are glued to the ground. And I also have a feeling that I haven't had since I was a small child. And that is, I'd like to run home and jump in bed and pull a quilt over my head."

"Hush, Matt, it's moving, and it's sliding away from the tree."

"I think it's a giant dragon," Matt declared.

"I thought all dragons breathed fire," Josh whispered.

"It's a dragon all right," Matt said.

"Oh, I hope not. Dragons were the most awful monsters of the ancient world. Is that not so?"

"That is so, but it would be a most astonishing thing if one had survived and was living here at Hell Hole Swamp."

"Are all dragons evil?" Josh asked.

"Not only evil, but destructive," Matt explained.

Josh was suddenly transfixed, and his brother noticed it.

"Are you in a swoon?" Matt asked.

"No. I've just made a startling discovery."

"Well, what is it? Don't keep secrets from me."

"You said that all dragons are evil and destructive. If that is true, then the green creature is not a dragon."

"What are you trying to tell me? Be specific," Matt said crossly.

"That is *not* a dragon," Josh said with authority.

"How do you know?"

"Because he is smiling."

"Then we're getting away from here!" Matt screamed. "Throw down that raccoon and run!"

"I'm not leaving the raccoon," Josh said, but just at that moment he lost his grip, and the animal slipped from his hands and scampered into the swamp.

For just an instant, Josh stood very still, not certain whether his mind was telling him to run away or try to rescue the raccoon.

Noticing his brother's hesitation, Matt yelled, "Josh! Are you mad? Leave the raccoon. That creature is coming for us!"

Matt and Josh turned and ran as fast as they could for a few moments. Finally, Josh stopped to catch his breath. Pain stabbed him in the chest, and he realized he had run so fast and gasped for breath so hard that he had to relax for a minute. While he was resting, he squinted his eyes in the direction of the swamp. "Matt, do you see what I see?"

"Yes."

"It isn't a dragon, is it?"

"No. It's a lizard, but it's the largest one in the world, I'm sure of it."

"He's as big as you are, Matt," Josh said as his eyes took in the monster, standing on his two hind legs.

"If he's as big as I am, then he's six feet tall."

"He's *seven* feet tall as sure as my name's Joshua Bondurant."

Matt was thinking back on all they had seen and thinking ahead of their return home, wondering what they would say if their mother asked them where they had been. It was a real possibility that she would question them on where they had been and what they had done during the hours they had been away from home. "Do you think we should tell anyone about this?"

"Have you lost your senses, Matt? We would never be allowed to come back here if anyone knew what happened today."

"You don't think for a second that we're going to come back here, do you?" Matt asked.

"You don't think for a second I'd *not* come back here,

do you?" Josh retorted. "Look closely at the lizard and you'll see that he is holding the little raccoon in his hands. If you think I'd leave that little helpless animal there with that monster, your brain has flown all the way to the moon. I'm going back to Hell Hole Swamp tomorrow, and I hope you'll go with me."

4

THAT NIGHT, WITH THE LAMPS gleaming brightly inside the mansion where he lived, Josh felt safe, but a curious thought did cross his mind. *Could that lizard be outside watching him?* It was absurd, he decided, although the reptile did possess certain gifts, like blending in with the surroundings so that no one on earth could detect his presence, and he could smile. Josh didn't doubt that the lizard had smiled at him, and anyone with a grain of sense knew that lizards could *not* smile.

Hell Hole Swamp was the lizard's domain, but something vague nagged at Josh. Finally, he walked into the drawing room, went to a ceiling-to-floor window, and pulled back a curtain. The outside was black velvet. There were likely many creatures outside, and though he couldn't see them they could surely see him, standing at the window, in the lamplight. He walked across the entrance hallway into the dining room and again looked out. There was nothing but darkness. Standing there he wondered if the lizard would dare eat the little raccoon. Surely not, but still...

Josh went to the library, where he could usually find his father during the evening hours.

"I wonder if lizards eat raccoons?" Josh innocently asked his father. He knew he would get an answer as his father never hesitated to respond to any questions his sons asked, and he always explained every detail as thoroughly as possible. It was one way of furthering the education of his children.

Mr. Bondurant removed his spectacles, put them on a table, and rubbed his eyes. "Son, it's funny you'd ask that question," he said, now looking at Josh. "Matthew just came to the library and searched for any book we have on reptiles. What's the sudden interest?"

"Oh nothing," Josh said, trying to make light of the situation. "We were walking today and saw a lizard, and I guess we just talked about it." That much was the truth, Josh was thinking. He hadn't lied, but he hadn't exactly told his father the whole truth.

"You remember some of the little raccoons that we have raised to maturity?" Mr. Bondurant asked.

"Sure."

"We fed one or two of them with a medicine dropper and later your mother put milk in a bottle, and still later, they ate scraps from the table. But if they had lived in the wild, they would have eaten crayfish, things like that. It's the same with lizards. In their native environment they would eat insects and small animals, but they certainly wouldn't eat anything as large as a raccoon." Mr. Bondurant looked at his son and said gently, "Lizards are different from snakes in many ways, and certainly one of them is their choice of foods. Lizards have much less interesting diets than snakes, and I don't think a raccoon would be on their bill of fare."

"Thanks, Father." Josh turned to go, and as he left the room he was thinking that usually his father's explanations counted for everything, and this would have been perfect for an ordinary lizard, but the one he had seen at Hell Hole Swamp was anything but ordinary, and his habits would not be ordinary either. It was quite possible, Josh believed, that the monster at Hell Hole Swamp would eat a small raccoon. On his way to his room, he tapped on Matt's door and poked his head in. Matt was reading by the light of three candles. "You think that lizard would eat the raccoon?" Josh asked.

Matt laid his book aside. "Jiminy! I don't know. I'd say that lizard is the closest thing to being prehistoric than anything we've ever encountered."

Josh shrugged his shoulders. "Could be. But I intend to learn a lot more about him." Josh walked across the carpet and looked at some of the books his twin was consulting. There was a book on lacertians, which from the information on the cover was about lizards, geckos, and chameleons. Another volume dealt with reptilians, specifically dragons, snakes, and crocodiles. "Mercy. You should find anything you need to know in those volumes."

"But it doesn't work that way. There's nothing here about a reptile such as the one that we almost got tangled up with." Matt pushed all the books to the back of the table. "You think it's safe to go back to Hell Hole Swamp tomorrow?"

"Safe or not, *I'm* going. And I'm going to bed early to hasten tomorrow."

Matt yawned. "Count me in."

Josh went to his room across the hall and went to bed, but sleep didn't come quickly. As he lay on the soft feather mattress, his eyes staring in the darkness, he pictured the lizard, standing on two hind feet, holding the furry raccoon. Suddenly it seemed like a dream, and Josh wondered if it had actually happened as he was now seeing it. The lizard standing on his hind feet and holding the abandoned animal was the last image on Josh's mind before he fell into slumber. The next morning, it took a few moments for the thoughts of the reptile to catch his attention. Suddenly he remembered what had happened yesterday, and he threw on his clothes in a hurry.

"What do you think we'll see today?" Josh asked as he and Matt skipped toward the fork in the road where the Lydia Oak stood.

"Who's to say? After what happened yesterday, *anything* could unfold."

"You make it sound so creepy."

"It *is* creepy. That lizard has probably opened his jaws

and swallowed the raccoon, and he may be all the way to California by this time."

"Oh, Matt. How can you go on so?"

"I'm *not* going on so, as you say," Matt answered crossly. "You're the one who's going on so, and that's because you're so fond of animals. It's going to kill you if you don't rescue that raccoon, and I'd say you stand about a chance in a million of doing that."

"I doubt that," Josh responded.

Just then the Lydia Oak came into view and the boys raced each other to the tree. Josh arrived first and sat down. When Matt flopped down beside him, Josh asked, "What did you learn from those books you read last night?"

"Not much, I'm afraid, that would apply to the monster we saw yesterday. But I did find out that lizards can play tricks."

"What kind of tricks?"

"Playing tricks is one of their defenses. They're good bluffers. They can swell up, hiss, and do all sorts of things with their tails," Matt explained.

"Like what?"

Matt stood up, got a twig, and began chewing on it. He was glancing toward The Shadows when he said, "Some lizards can pull themselves away from their tails."

"Oh, don't expect me to believe that!"

"Believe it or not. It's your choice. But it's true that a lizard's tail is twice as long as its body, and as brittle as, as..." Matt removed the twig from his mouth. "As brittle as this stick." He broke the twig in half and casually threw it away. "If an enemy seizes the lizard's tail, the animal can pull its body away from the tail and crawl to safety."

"And what happens to the tail, yarnspinner?'"

"It's *not* a yarn, Josh, and you'd better clear that space you call a brain and listen to what I'm saying. To answer your question, the disengaged tail just keeps on wiggling, and I don't care if you believe it or not. I think the heat has gotten to you."

"Maybe so," Josh said, thinking that it *was* warm. Each

year as spring came on, so did the heat, and the people on the plantation could feel it increasing from one day to the next. But it never bothered them too much, as they had been born to the climate of the South Carolina Low Country, and they liked summer better than any other part of the year. Josh and Matt found summer to be a time of adventure and discovery, and there was no end to the discoveries on the plantation. A portion of The Bond extended along the Cooper River, and there were always many vessels traveling that waterway. The twins' father also owned a plantation that was on the ocean, and sometimes large sea creatures washed up on the sand. Once, after a terrible hurricane, the sand was covered in whales, and after Mr. Bondurant discovered the phenomenon he went home for his sons so they could see something they would never again witness. As they walked on the backs of the whales, their father said, "You will always have a legacy that other people don't have. It's very unlikely that you'll ever meet a man who can boast that he has walked on whales." Josh, now thinking back on the day he had walked on whales, suddenly felt sad. But not wanting to let on to his twin that he was already homesick for his plantation home even before he left for England, he said nothing, but suggested that they get on with their journey.

Again walking that fearsome roadway known as The Shadows, Josh and Matt talked about the trees and plants. Leaves were in several shades of green, as well as some mosses that were ground-cover growth, rather than Spanish moss that swung from tree limbs. After a while, they came to a tree by the side of the lane that looked as though it were standing on stilts.

"Well, Brain, explain that," Josh needled his brother.

Matt looked at the unusual tree for a few minutes. He thought back on his studies of botany, and then he had the answer. "When that tree was just getting started, it grew over a fallen log, which separated the tree's trunk into two parts. After the tree had grown taller, the log rotted away, leaving a hole in the trunk of the tree. That is how the split trunk took on the shape of stilts."

"We don't call you 'Brain' for nothing."

"Don't let it get to you," Matt said, his eyes now focusing on the forest. He changed the subject. "Dangers lurk there."

"Pardon?"

"There are pools of quicksand, for one thing," Matt explained.

"Father says a pool of quicksand is the most life-threatening thing on the plantation."

"It can kill you before you know what's happening," Matt agreed.

"Like drowning."

"Worse."

"I guess you're referring to the story about the man on his horse that trotted into a pool of quicksand, and when the horse bowed his head, the rider was thrown over the horse's head and within minutes not even a ripple was there to show where they had gone down."

Matt shook his head. "It's too horrible to contemplate."

"You think I should get a stick and punch around as we walk? Just in case?" Josh asked. Without awaiting an answer, he ran to the side of the lane and reached for a stick, but it wiggled away from him. "Hey! I thought that was a stick, but it was a snake. Sometimes snakes are so nearly the same color of the ground you can't see them."

"Keep your hands in your pockets," Matt cautioned.

Just then the twins came to the last stretch of road, and they knew that the swamp was around the bend.

"Afraid?" Josh asked.

"I'd never admit it," his twin answered.

Moments later the awesome scene they had witnessed the day before stretched before them, and the boys stood motionless. They left the road and moved into the forest, until Josh touched Matt's arm. "See what I see?"

"I presume you're talking about that shape that is moving slowly under the slime?" Matt asked softly.

"Is it a whale?" Josh asked, being careful not to shout.

"It couldn't possibly be a whale. They live in the ocean."

"Then what is it?"

"How would I know?"

Josh's heart thudded. "Matt, that's the lizard, under the slime."

Matt studied the pool for a few seconds. "No, it's not the lizard, but only the reptile's tail. Look on the bank."

Josh's eyes followed the shape billowing under the water to the waterline, and the lizard was lolling on the roots of a cypress tree. "He looks almost asleep, but he's gently moving his tail," Josh observed.

"I can't believe this," Matt said. "Look at his hands. In all the reading I did on lizards, I read of none that had three fingers on each hand."

"This one does, and he's still holding the raccoon."

"What're you looking at?" Matt asked as Josh scrutinized some overhanging limbs.

Josh was quiet for a moment, thinking. Finally, he said, "I believe I can make it over the tributaries and get around there and grab the raccoon."

Matt took a deep breath, put his hands on his hips, and turned his back on his brother. "Now I know your senses have taken leave of you." He turned back to face Josh. "That would be suicide."

"Hold still," Josh said, analyzing the situation.

"I'm having no part of this. The last thing I want to see is a lizard having my brother for dinner. And I'm *not* going to allow you to do it. If you'd think about it, you'd realize that no animal on earth is worth the life of a human being."

"I'm *not* going to lose my life." Josh ran to the first tree, caught hold of a limb above his head, and pulled himself up, his feet dangling in the air.

"Josh, stop this. It's madness."

Josh looked down over a shoulder. "I'm not going all the way around." In his logical mind, he was not frightened of a confrontation with the lizard. A reptile that had smiled wasn't mean enough to attack a human being.

"That does it. I'm going home." Matt turned and started walking away.

Josh was now up in the tree, making his way through

some scratchy twigs. "And if I need help, there won't be any around," he said in a loud whisper.

Matt turned and stared at his brother. Josh's words stabbed Matt in the heart. Although the mission was taking on increasing horror for Matt, he said, "I must be mad, but I'm not willing to leave you to your own weak defenses. I thought you were a bona fide Bondurant, but you're like no other one I've ever known. If you don't care any more for your life than to throw it away, well, that's one thing, but it seems to me you'd at least think of Mother and Father."

"They'll never know about this," Josh whispered back.

"They'll know about it when I go home and tell them you're in the belly of a giant lizard."

"Use that brain of yours, Matt. You know I'm going to take care of myself."

"You haven't one sliver of self-preservation!"

Josh dropped down from the tree after he had crossed over the inlet. "Come on over," he called softly. "You can get a better look at the lizard from here."

Matt's eyes scanned the swamp. His concern for his brother mounted. He threw Josh a quick, puzzled glance, and knew that he had to go with him. There was no such thing as one twin abandoning another. Matt could see that Josh didn't know what he was getting into, and Josh expected him to be an eager and willing partner in this—this—game of chance. Matt bit his lip. "If one twin dies, both may as well go together."

Matt had to jump three times before he could reach the limb that Josh had caught the first time, but when he reached it, he fairly flew as he picked his way across the water, as he wanted to get this adventure over and done with.

"I'm going over one more tributary," Josh whispered back, "so that I can see every nook and cranny of this swamp."

"You said we could assess the situation from there," Matt objected.

But Josh was already flying across the inlet. He hadn't

given a thought to making a quick getaway if something frightful happened.

Matt dropped down to the other side of the inlet, and pulled himself up to the limb of another tree. "This surely is the worst day of my life," he groaned.

Josh had now dropped to the ground, and his eyes were searching every inch of the scene.

Just then everything became deathly still, the same as yesterday.

"Listen," Josh said. "Listen to the quiet."

"Let's get out of here," Matt called.

"Hang on."

Matt had an excellent view of the lizard from the tree in which he was standing. "The lizard is pulling himself up," he whispered as he dropped himself out of the tree.

The tail was now out of the water and the lizard was up on his two hind feet. The reptile turned toward Josh and held out a hand. The raccoon was holding to one of the fingers.

"I believe I can get that raccoon," Josh said. "If I were there right now I'd grab him and climb a tree so high that the lizard couldn't reach me."

"And you'd probably have to stay up there the rest of your life. Don't even think of such a thing," Matt scowled. "I always knew you were obsessed with small animals, but the raccoon isn't worth the danger we're in."

Just then wisps of that thick and peculiar mist that often rise from plantation swamps floated up from the slime, like a million tiny ghosts. "Fog is coming, Josh, and you're coming home with me or I'll never go anywhere with you again," Matt said. So dense was the fog that Matt could see no more than a few yards of escape route before him.

Josh knew that his brother meant business. It was true that swamp fog could envelop a person and cause the individual to lose all sense of direction. "All right," Josh agreed. "We'll go home, but mark this on your brain—tomorrow I'm coming back to this place, and when I leave

I intend to have the raccoon. I'd rescue him today if the fog wasn't drifting up."

"Hurry up!" Matt hissed. "If you don't hurry we'll get closed in by the fog, and there's no telling whose sharp, scratchy claws will grab you and hold you for hours." Right now Matt was thinking that his twin was as stubborn as an ox. If any of the oxen on the plantation chose to stop in their tracks, they did so, and no amount of coaxing would spur them on. Matt climbed back in the tree to cross over the inlet and head for home.

"I'm only afraid of the claws of the fog, and not of any unseen creatures," Josh answered as he pushed back limbs and made his way through a thicket of thorny foliage. Inch-high fog ghosts were filling the air around him.

"No! Oh heavens, no!" Matt screamed.

"What's wrong?" Josh stood still in terror.

At the very spot where Matt was just about to lower himself on the bank of a tributary lay a great, black alligator, his mouth open and his teeth white and sharp. As Josh and Matt watched, the alligator snapped his mouth shut, placed his chin on the swamp mud, and obviously made himself comfortable for a long nap.

Josh looked around for another means of escape, but there was nothing to his liking. The lizard stood regally behind him, the raccoon still clinging to a finger. "This is *real* trouble."

"There is no place to flee," Matt cried. "And the fog is still rising. We cannot go forward and we can't go backward." He glanced back at the lizard, who was taking in the drama. For the first time, Matt noticed that the lizard's eyes were blood red. When exposed to light, they grew bright and lustrous like a cat's.

5

MATT COULDN'T REMEMBER ever being so afraid. "Mother and Father told us never to come to Hell Hole Swamp," he remarked with a hint of accusation in his voice.

"You're blaming me for it," Josh said.

"Blame is unimportant in this predicament," Matt answered. His mind was working frantically, trying to think back on all of the dangerous situations he'd been in earlier in his life and how he had resolved them. But nothing had ever compared to the danger he now faced. If he dropped down from the tree, he'd go right into the jaws of the alligator. And if he worked his way backward, he'd go into the three-fingered hands of the lizard. Each alternative was as perilous as the other. The whole thing was so bizarre that it made him feel weak. But he had to brace up to the situation, as the twins *had* to get away from the swamp.

Just then a thought struck Matt. If he and Josh could make their way to the road by climbing trees and going from one tree to another in the manner of a squirrel, they could go through the forest until they reached the road. "I think I've figured out how we can get out of this."

"If you know of any way we can get out of this mess, then please spit it out," Josh said nastily. He'd always been the headstrong son, and it was showing.

"Don't come unfolded now," Matt admonished. "I think our only chance of escape is through the trees. I'm going to see if I can make it from one tree to another until we can jump down and run for The Shadows."

"But that undergrowth is like spikes."

Matt realized that Josh's statement was true. If they fell on a clump of Spanish sword they could be impaled. It was an agonizing thought, but it was their only chance. "We've got to give it a try," Matt said as he looked around for the largest tree he could find. If ever he needed a giant live oak tree it was now, because the limbs of live oaks were long, and they extended into other trees in the forest. "I think I see a live oak, but the fog is closing in, and we've got to move quickly." Matt started on his way through the limbs. "If this doesn't save us, we're lost forever." He hoped Josh was coming behind him.

The twins didn't talk to each other was they cringed and inched their way forward, sometimes climbing, other times kneeling, and now and then moving on their stomachs as they pulled themselves along on a limb. Now and then Matt would stop, look around, and then turn and go in a slightly different direction. Josh followed him, never disagreeing with a decision. Finally, they could see the opening ahead. It was the roadway, and when they dropped from the last limb, they were totally exhausted.

The twins caught their breath as they stood for a moment, gazing at the dense growth and slimy water bathed in gauzy white fog.

"Do you believe this place has some sort of power over us?" Josh asked.

Matt took a deep breath. "Not exactly. We have a certain will and intellect, but we do possess certain weaknesses, and it's entirely possible that in a moment of weak-kneed vulnerability we were cast into a spell by this strange place."

Josh thought about Matt's philosophical words. "Something keeps us coming back, and that's for sure."

"I think it's not power at all, but fear and hope. A philosopher once said that fear cannot be without hope nor hope without fear. Perhaps we fear this place so much that we hope we can overcome it."

"For you maybe," Josh answered, "but my only desire is to remove the raccoon from the fingers of the lizard, and after that, Hell Hole Swamp will hold no power, fear, hope, or anything else over my head."

Matt held still for a moment, thinking. "There is some sort of violence here that I can't see or touch," he said finally. "But I can feel it. Sometimes it feels hot, and there is so much noise that it sounds like dogs scrapping. Other times it's cool, and as quiet as fog."

As they talked about it, the boys decided that many dangers lurked in the swamp. Everything there was alive, and it wasn't beyond belief that some unseen threats skulked in the shadows or under the slime.

"The moss hanging from the limbs is alive, and it grows and changes," Matt observed. "Even the slime on the water has a life."

"When I free the raccoon I'll never come here again," Josh said, turning toward home.

Walking with the sun on their backs, the twins discussed the marvel that their parents had not discovered their attraction to Hell Hole Swamp. Both Mr. and Mrs. Bondurant were busy with their own interests, and they reposed full trust in their twins. Had it not been the time of the planting of rice seed, a time that required the full attention of the master of a plantation, Mr. Bondurant would surely have ridden one of his fine horses in the vicinity and gotten a glimpse of his sons. However, as he was spending so much time in the rice fields, Matt and Josh felt perfectly safe from detection, and the daily visits there were the focal points of the days that were now noticeably longer. The next morning on their way to the swamp, their spirits were lighter, and there was no talk of the swamp holding any force over them. But just before Matt and Josh turned into the bend, they sensed a difference.

"Something's wrong," Matt declared.

"What is it?"

"I don't know. But it's like a—a—well, a flutter."

Matt and Josh slowed down and walked gingerly around the bend. Something *had* changed, as the water was covered in ducks, each one, it seemed, fluttering its wings, trying to make room for itself on the surface of the water.

"What are they doing, Matt?"

"Eating. These ducks are on their way north for the summer, and they are feasting on the slime."

"But they wouldn't eat *that*!"

An attentive expression spread over Matt's face. He went to the edge of the water, and dozens of brown ducks took to the air in a swarm. Matt pinched off a bit of the green stuff floating on the water. "This isn't slime, it's the tiniest leaves you ever looked at."

Josh was now pinching off a piece, and he held it toward a stab of sunlight. "It *is* leaves, but I'd have guessed it was slime."

"It's the very same color as the stuff that collects on stagnant water," Matt explained. "I'd say this growth must be in the seaweed family, but this water isn't salt water, so that doesn't make sense."

"Then what is it?" Josh asked.

"I suppose it is some kind of green algae that ducks eat."

Just then Josh thought about the lizard and his eyes scanned the swamp. "Wonder where the lizard is."

"No sign of him," Matt answered.

"The raccoon's not here either," Josh said, instantly becoming furious. "If I find out that the lizard abandoned the raccoon, or ate him, I'm going to tell Father, and he'll shoot the reptile."

"Don't tell Father anything about this," Matt cautioned.

"Well, that lizard's not here," Josh snapped. "And I'm going to search for him, even if I have to go all the way around the swamp."

"That is one of your worst decisions," Matt said.

"Watch me. Here I go." Josh reached up for a limb and worked his way over the inlet.

"See any alligators?"

"Don't worry about alligators! Come on."

Matt shook his head in a gesture of futility and reached up for a limb.

"That lardy-dardy lizard is going to get what's coming to him," Josh called back.

"And you think *you're* the one who can give it to him?"

"Who else? You don't seem to have any ideas."

"Sure hope we don't have to make a quick exodus," Matt said, trying to envision every eventuality.

"If we do, it won't be the first time," Josh shot back. "Don't give up now."

Some of the ducks had flown away; the swamp was dark and murky. Josh stopped to survey the passage up ahead, and he concluded that the going would get easier. "Matt," he called back toward his brother, "the trees are bigger now, and the limbs are long and substantial. It's not bad at all."

Matt didn't catch up with Josh until they were about a third of the way around the swamp. "I don't know where that lizard is," Josh said, "and if we never see him again and mentioned it to somebody, they'd never believe we saw him in the first place."

"And if we tried to describe the creature, we'd be accused of talking about a dinosaur."

"But no dinosaur was any scarier than that lizard," Josh stated. "You think the ducks frightened him away?"

"I don't think anything could frighten the lizard, but he's gone."

Josh shinnied up the next tree to the first limb, where he stood, holding on to the limb above him. "Matt. Oh, Matt!"

"What is it?"

Josh jumped to the ground, fell, and rolled nearly into the pool. Several ducks flew away. Scrambling up, Josh blurted out, "The biggest snake I've ever seen is wound around a huge limb."

Matt helped Josh up. "Look very carefully. That is not a snake."

"Then what in the name of heaven is it?" Josh asked.

"It's the lizard."

Josh let his eyes follow the limb all the way across the next tributary, and Matt was right. The lizard straddled the limb, and his tail, which was longer than his body, was wrapped around the limb.

"Matt," Josh whispered, "he's looking at us. And he's got the raccoon."

"And he's precisely above us," Matt answered.

6

The long, sharp, shiny tail slowly unwound, and in a flash it went into the air and came to rest on the lizard's back. The green creature began to back up, coming closer to Matt and Josh, and the raccoon was holding onto one of the lizard's fingers.

Not taking his eyes off the monster, Josh murmured, "That raccoon thinks the lizard's his mother."

"What are we going to do?" Matt asked, terror cracking his voice.

"I'm going to try to grab the raccoon, and when I get him, you be ready to fly as fast as you can."

Matt pictured in his mind squirrels running on the limbs, flying from one tree to the next until they had traveled a long distance. "We're not squirrels."

"Well, you'd better run like one," Josh said, waiting to see where the lizard settled down.

But the rogue revolved around so that he could slide his tail into the water, and just as it had happened before, everything in the region became restless. And then all was quiet. Birds and insects hushed, and even the ducks rocked gently and quietly on the water. Matt staggered back a step.

Suddenly the lizard brought his tail from the water, raised it high into the air, and with a brisk flip it cracked the air like lightning. When Matt and Josh looked, the ducks had disappeared.

"Josh, look at the water. It's clear of slime."

"The ducks have eaten all of it."

Josh and Matt now faced the lizard. "Do we dare try to escape?" Matt asked.

"He's not harming us," Josh said. "Give me time to get the raccoon."

"Don't risk it," Matt cautioned.

"Try to be friendly to the lizard," Josh said. "I'm waiting for an opportunity to grab the animal."

"You're asking for whatever happens to us," Matt commented. "Let the lizard keep the raccoon."

"Not on your life," Josh replied. "I'm close enough now to touch the lizard."

"Look at that face," Matt said, and broke Josh's train of thought. "It's the face of a lizard, but it has a 'boy' quality too."

"How do you mean?"

"His eyes look as though they can comprehend things, like the fact that we are nearly scared out of our skin. And the mouth *does* have a faint smile on it."

"His eyes are red and searching," Josh added.

"An appropriate description," Matt commented. "They seem as searing and searching as the eyes of that famous poet."

"Who?"

"Edgar Allan Poe. Have you noticed the eyes in his pictures in some of his books of tales?"

"I can't say that I have," Josh said, a little morosely, as he had just been reminded in a subtle way that Matt was the reader in the family.

"I believe," Matt began, and then hesitated as he looked deeply into the lizard's eyes.

"What? What do you believe?"

"It seems to me that if we showed any terror, we might be in for trouble. But as long as we stand our ground, and don't rush off in haste, the creature is going to study us, much in the same manner as we are studying him."

"I have no intention of studying him," Josh said. "All I

want is to get my hands on the raccoon, and then you'll see me fly home so fast I'll only be a blur to you."

"If this creature intended to harm us he could have done it by now," Matt reasoned, ignoring his brother's statement. "But maybe I am going mad. If my mind were in perfect order, I'd be getting away from this swamp right this minute."

"How big would you say he is?" Josh asked.

Matt looked at the lizard from the head to the end of the tail. "Comparing him to the height of the trees here, I'd say he is as long as any of father's seagoing vessels."

"As long as that?"

"The green skin looks to be as hard as stone," Matt noted. The boys also observed how it seemed to be made up of thousands of small prisms reflecting the slants of the sun through the trees.

"I'm going to touch that skin."

"It's your own decision. But if you do, don't display any fear," Matt cautioned.

Josh reached out a hand, then withdrew it uncertainly. Slowly he extended his hand again. Just at that moment the lizard moved a hand toward Josh, but the raccoon was in the other hand, which the lizard kept away from the boys.

"I'm going to touch his finger, Matt."

"Are you sure?"

Josh moved closer to the reptile. Although he attempted to smile, the corners of his mouth quivered.

"Remember, don't show fear."

Josh smiled again and reached out. He touched the lizard's finger, then quickly withdrew his hand.

"What did it feel like?" Matt asked.

"Slick. Cold."

Matt shrugged his shoulders. "*I* can't touch him."

"You can if you want to be friends," Josh said, again reaching out to the monster. "Do you think he'll give us the raccoon?"

"No. He's not letting us get close to the animal."

"Why?"

"Because the lizard thinks the raccoon is his, and the raccoon now has taken a liking to the lizard."

"They *have* taken to each other," Josh agreed. "But I'm going to try to separate them."

"If you value your life, you'll do no such thing."

"Just watch me." Josh held out *his* hand, and the lizard touched it, with one of the three fingers on his hand. Josh decided to go a step farther, and he pointed to the raccoon.

Suddenly the lizard backed away, a look of irritation on his face.

"You went too far," Matt said. "Now you've upset the lizard."

"Do you think he understood what I meant?" Josh asked.

"I think he understood it perfectly. He knows that you want the raccoon, and he's not going to give the animal up. You were to the point of making friends with the lizard, but now you have annoyed him. It was a terrible mistake."

Josh took a big breath and exhaled deeply.

"Let the lizard keep the raccoon, Josh!" his brother reprimanded. "He is probably being a better mother to the raccoon than you could be. This is nature's way of giving the animal a feeling of security, and sort of den, and you're trying to upset nature. You can't do that."

"How long is it going to take you to understand that *I* am going to get the raccoon away from the lizard?"

Matt shook his head. "Let's go, if we can."

"What do you mean by that remark?"

"Now that you have made the lizard mad, he might decide to keep *us* here with him."

"Don't be a silly goose!"

"Josh, remember this. Lizards are wild animals, and wild animals are not friendly to humans. Come away."

"*This* animal would be friendly if you'd give him a chance," Josh said. "You wouldn't even touch him."

Suddenly, Josh moved close to the lizard and gently

touched one of the three fingers. "Going," Josh said, as he pointed toward home.

Matt was climbing a tree and paying no attention to Josh. Just then Matt noticed an alligator, pulling his heavy black torso up on the bank. "Josh, we're stuck. We can't go down from this tree as an alligator is on the bank, and we are too far from the road to go through the trees. What are we going to do?"

"Beats me!"

Matt and Josh stood perfectly still, Matt in a tree and Josh standing by the trunk, contemplating the situation. Finally, Matt said, "You'd better climb this tree. That 'gator could get to you and snap off a hand before you could yell for help."

Josh quickly climbed the tree, where he sat down on a limb. Matt sat beside him. "We may be in for a long wait," Matt said.

Just then the lizard backed his tail into the water and moved it in the direction of the alligator, still lying on the swamp bank. As quick as a flash of lightning, the lizard brought his tail from the water and cracked it over the alligator, who moved into the pool and was out of sight so quickly there wasn't even a ripple left.

"Matt, the lizard scared off the alligator so we can go home!" Josh exclaimed.

"I realize it. Do you think I'm stupid?"

"No, but nobody in the world would believe a lizard did that."

"I'm not sure *I* believe it," Matt answered. "If I hadn't seen it with my own eyes I know I wouldn't believe it."

"Let's get out of here," Josh said.

After the boys reached the road, they looked back. The lizard was, as usual, standing on his two hind feet and holding the raccoon.

"If ever a lizard smiled," Matt said, "that one is smiling."

"Going," Josh called, pointing toward home. "I'll see you tomorrow, lizard."

Josh suggested that they race to the Lydia Oak, and when they reached the oak tree and stopped for a rest they heard hoofs, coming toward them on Ropemaker's Lane.

"Who could that be?" Josh asked.

"I don't know, but if it's Father, let me handle it," Matt said.

Josh bowed from the waist. "I yield to the Brain."

Mr. Bondurant pranced his stallion to a stop. "What are you boys doing here near Hell Hole Swamp?"

Josh looked at Matt.

Matt racked his brain to try to come up with a plausible explanation that didn't include any information regarding the lizard. Like Josh, he was becoming attached to the reptile.

"I'm awaiting an answer," Mr. Bondurant persisted.

"Father," Matt uttered, "when we get to Cambridge, we'll be expected to write papers on certain subjects, as a part of our education."

"True," Mr. Bondurant agreed.

"We are studying the wildlife of this area," Matt said truthfully, and added, "and trying to locate the sphinx you have told us about," not quite so truthfully.

Josh had question marks in his eyes as he gazed at his twin.

"Keep your mouth shut," Matt mumbled out of a corner of his mouth. "I'll explain later."

7

THAT EVENING MR. BONDURANT had arranged some papers on the desk in the library before he summoned his sons. When they came into the room, their senses were alert, awaiting any confrontation about being in the vicinity of Hell Hole Swamp. Matt and Josh knew that their father wouldn't have one iota of compassion for them if he knew they had been going there. Each of the twins had vowed to the other that there would be no talk of their scheming to free the raccoon from the lizard, and in fact they would not reveal the presence of the lizard at all.

Mr. Bondurant smiled, and his sons were at once reassured and devoid of anxiety. "I have a large degree of respect for you, Matthew and Joshua, for thinking of your studies at Cambridge, and making preparation for them now, and I want you to know that I shall help you in any way I can. But first, let me once again warn you to stay away from Hell Hole Swamp. It's a dangerous place and I forbid you to go there."

If ever a gigantic lizard had been seen there, now was the time to find out, Matt concluded. Trusting that he wasn't giving any information away, he asked, "Father, may I ask you something?"

"Of course, Matthew. What do you want to know?"

"I have two subjects to explore on the plantation before I leave for England—plantation reptiles and the sphinx.

I'm wondering if you've ever seen any unusual reptile, such as a lizard, in the area of Hell Hole Swamp."

"That's a good question, Matt," Josh said, behaving as though Matt had only now thought of such a thing.

"I have a natural distaste for Hell Hole Swamp," Mr. Bondurant responded in a way that at once put Josh and Matt at ease. Their father didn't suspect a thing!

"I am repelled and irritated just to picture in my mind that despicable place."

"Why do you have such contempt for it, Father?" Matt asked.

"Much violence has erupted there. The bodies of two men who were murdered on this plantation were found in that pool, and the men had been tortured. Gangsters and other people of no natural integrity have been known to hide there. But as this place is on my plantation, I go there occasionally and look around. As I think back on it now, I have never seen any unusual reptile there. Of course alligators are in the pool, but they are not unusual, and I do not recall having seen any sort of lizard in the region."

Matt wanted to look at Josh, but he restrained himself. "That's interesting, Father, that the swamp is not a natural habitat for lizards."

"The swamp would not be a habitat for lizards, in my opinion," Mr. Bondurant said, "and if an unusual reptile were found there, I would judge that it had simply adopted Hell Hole Swamp as a temporary home rather than a permanent one."

Josh sucked in his breath in delighted surprise. If the lizard didn't live in the swamp, then he and Matt had been fortunate to discover him during the time he was there.

Matt gave his father a penetrating look and asked, "If one actually did discover an extremely large lizard there, then one could assume that it was just passing through the region. Is that correct?" He said no more, as he was cautiously feeling his way with his father.

"In all likelihood. And now, let's get to the sphinx," Mr.

Bondurant said, changing the subject. He smoothed out an ancient map on the desk, and the boys got up and stood where they could see the map. Mr. Bondurant adjusted the lamp for a clearer view.

"I know very little about the sphinx, Father," Josh admitted. "What *is* a sphinx?"

Mr. Bondurant leaned back in his chair. "A sphinx is an imaginary creature of ancient myths. The Egyptians, the Greeks, and peoples of the Near East all had stories about such a creature. According to some stories, the sphinx had a human head, the body of a lion, the tail of a serpent, and the wings of a bird."

"Isn't there a statue of a great sphinx in Egypt?" Matt asked.

Mr. Bondurant looked at Matt with interest, a smile playing around his gentle mouth. "You are perceptive, Matt. The great sphinx in Egypt stares with sightless eyes across the desert, as it has for thousands of years." Mr. Bondurant reached for a book that he had removed from a shelf and laid on the desk. He opened it to a marker that he had previously placed in the book, and pointed to a sketch of the Egyptian sphinx.

Matt read a description of the statue from the book. "The great sphinx that stands near the great pyramid in Egypt is one of the most famous monuments in the world. Its head and body are carved from solid rock, and the paws and legs are built of stone blocks. The face is believed to be a portrait of the pharaoh who built it. No one knows exactly which pharaoh built the sphinx."

Matt stopped reading, and Josh read a couple of sentences. "The great sphinx is 240 feet long and about 66 feet high. The width of its face measures 13 feet 8 inches." Josh looked at his father and asked, "What was the sphinx used for?"

"There were sphinxes in Greece as well as Egypt, and they were supposed to represent some god, but we believe in another God, the one who is our Father in Heaven."

"And what were the pyramids for?" Josh asked.

"They were tombs of rulers."

"And you have a map that shows a sphinx on this plantation, Father?" Matt asked.

Mr. Bondurant leaned forward quickly, staring at the map. His shoulders hunched over the desk as he focused his eyes on the drawing of the Cooper River and adjoining plantations. "This map was drawn in England," he said, "in the mid-1600s."

The map showed the Atlantic Ocean, Cooper and Ashley rivers, various inlets, and plantations, including The Bond. There were dozens of crooked tributaries, and other snakelike lines indicated creeks. Large expanses of seamarsh were indicated by little tufts of grass, each tuft consisting of three blades. All words were written in fancy script.

"Is the sphinx on the map, Father?" Josh wanted to know.

His father placed a finger on a line and carefully advanced the finger to a place indicated as the Cooper River.

Matt was about to burst with curiosity. "Do you see anything about the sphinx?"

And then they saw the words. Among the tufts of grass that indicated a large seamarsh were the words *tapia sphinx* in delicate handwriting.

"It's on the map! I see it! It's there in the marsh," Matt all but shouted. "I've got to locate it, and do further research on sphinxes, and write something of value."

"Is it *truly* there, Father?" Josh asked.

Mr. Bondurant leaned back and took a deep breath. "I have searched for it since the first time I saw the word on the map. Although I have never located it, I believe it is there. You can see that it was constructed of tabby."

"We have other tabby structures here," Matt said.

"That's correct," his father replied. "The most obvious example of tabby is our water cistern."

"Just what is tabby, Father?" Josh asked. "Although I've seen tabby I haven't really thought of how it is made."

"Tabby construction was very common with the Spaniards," Mr. Bondurant explained. "They built fortresses and churches of tabby, and there are some interesting tabby ruins on St. Helena Island." It was obvious to Mr. Bondurant that his sons were interested in what he was telling them. "I have experimented with tabby work off and on, and I think that probably the best results can be gained by mixing two buckets of gravel, one of slacked lime, and four buckets of raw oyster shells."

"And then what?" Josh asked.

"All of the ingredients should be put in a vat and stirred thoroughly until the mass reaches the right consistency. It is then poured in moulds and beaten down with a wooden mallet, but not enough, however, to crush up the shells—merely hard enough to press them firmly together. Two days at least should be allowed for drying."

"Is it as sturdy as the brick that comes from England as ballast in ships?" Matt queried.

"Absolutely. Many dwellings have been built of tabby, and for a one-story house, I would suggest that the walls at the bottom should be about ten inches thick and should taper up at the eaves to eight inches. Boards are used as moulds. When the first few feet of tabby have dried the boards are moved up and another mixture poured in. Cavities are left for sills and joists."

"What is the advantage of building with tabby?" Matt asked.

"They say that tabby construction, being mated to the soil, has advantages over other types of materials, and as you can see, it costs very little. Shells are on the seabeach for the taking, and lime can be made by burning the shells in kilns. Additionally, tabby buildings are well insulated against heat and cold, and it has certainly been proved that they last for generations."

"That explains why tabby was used in the construction of the sphinx, but *why* was the sphinx built in the first place?" Matt asked.

"If I knew the answer to that question, I'd probably know just where the sphinx is, if indeed it exists at all. It likely was a tomb for someone with an exaggerated sense of self-importance. On the other hand, the Spaniards could have built it simply as a monument. As I said, I've searched for it, but to no avail."

"Do you have any objection to our starting a search tomorrow?" Matt asked.

"None in the least. I'd like to see you boys locate it and write an essay about it. That should prove to be interesting to many people, even in future generations."

Matt looked at Josh. "Then we'll begin the pursuit in the morning."

Josh nodded.

Mr. Bondurant regarded his sons carefully, a shrewd look in his eyes. "I wish you all the success in the world. If there were any advice that I thought would be of help, I'd give it, but all I can think to tell you is that from the map it appears that the sphinx was built in the area of the brick towers."

"You mean the brick towers where the slaves stayed during the hurricanes?" Matt asked.

"Yes. My great-grandfather, the fifth Bondurant to live on this land, built those circular buildings for the safety of his workers. There were as many harsh hurricanes during the early years as now, and the slaves were safe in those buildings. But one important word of caution. Vines and other growth have claimed that part of the plantation, and snakes are common there. Watch your step."

"We'll be careful, Father," Matt said.

Later that night, as the twins made their way to their rooms upstairs, Matt made a solemn promise to his brother. If they gave three days of intense search to the discovery of the sphinx and found nothing, on the fourth day they would again go to Hell Hole Swamp and try to take the raccoon from the lizard.

8

THE NEXT MORNING Matt burst into life as though it were a song. As he slung his arms into the suspenders and pulled up his trousers he went from stanza to stanza, his spirits lifting to higher levels, leading to a crescendo as he burned with love for the project that thrilled him more than any he'd ever known. And last night Josh had promised to join him for three days in search of the sphinx before he insisted that they go to Hell Hole Swamp. If the two of them searched for three whole days, they could surely find the sphinx in that time!

For the first time in his life, Matt was testing his brain, *really* testing it. Whereas others had failed in locating the sphinx, he would succeed. The Spaniards, the first white men who came to these shores, built their first settlement, San Miguel de Gualdape, on the Waccamaw River. And when they found the Cooper River to their liking, they built a sphinx, which surely would have been in view of those traveling the river. Matt liked the second of his father's theories on the origin of the sphinx. Surely the Spaniards had built it. There were only a few places where the statue could be located, Matt believed, as the rice fields took up almost every inch of riverfront land, and if those people who carved out the rice fields had discovered the sphinx they would have revealed it. Consequently, the statue *had* to be in the vicinity of the circular brick buildings that had been used during hurricanes as shelters for slaves. When the twins arrived there, Matt would try to decide where the Spaniards would have built their monument.

"Don't forget that I am indulging you by participating in this defeating venture," Josh remarked when they were on their way.

"What are you talking about?" Matt asked in a hostile voice that indicated he wouldn't accept any insolence from his brother.

"It *is* defeating. If that sphinx can be found, it would have been discovered centuries ago."

"This project is *not* defeating," Matt said, his voice nearly freezing in his throat. "I went with you to Hell Hole Swamp, when rescuing that animal was the last thing of interest to me. And did you hear me complain? No. I even helped you several times when you were in trouble."

"So what?" A sneer disfigured Josh's face.

Matt stopped walking and faced his brother. "What is it? Didn't you agree to give me three days for this search and then we'd go back to Hell Hole Swamp?"

"That was in a moment of weakness. Now I'm wondering if the lizard will be there when we go back."

"The lizard will be there in three days, and you know it. The raccoon will also be there. Are you thinking of going back on our agreement?" Matt asked.

"Keep walking," Josh said, stepping ahead of his brother.

"Whew! I thought you could be trusted to live up to a promise."

"I'll live up to my promise, but that doesn't mean that I'm going to enjoy this fruitless search."

"Think about it for a minute. What if we actually *find* the sphinx? Just imagine what pleasure it would bring to Father. And I believe we will locate it within the three days."

"You do?" Josh asked, not really believing that it would be possible *ever* to find the sphinx.

"Of course I do. I believe we have a better chance of

locating the sphinx than of getting the raccoon away from the lizard."

"What are you saying? You don't believe that!"

"I *do* believe that. That lizard's not going to give up the only friend he has in this world. But that's not saying that I won't go back with you to Hell Hole Swamp and try to free him."

"Fair enough," Josh said. "I'll give you your three days, but then I'm going back to see the lizard."

"That was the agreement in the first place, and I plan to honor it. You are the one that seems to want to back out."

"All right, Brain, you have your three days, and I won't object any more."

"Well, let's put our minds to locating the sphinx. I don't think I've ever been so driven to do something in my entire life," Matt said. "I'm just bursting with energy to begin this project."

Just then the boys reached a summit where they could view the low-lying portion of the plantation. On a ridge in the distance, miles away, Mr. Bondurant sat on his stallion, taking it in. He often came to this place, where he could get a sweeping view of the fields that made him a millionaire. Never had a year come when the price for rice wasn't sky-high in England, and the rice fields at The Bond were perfect for production of the crop. Twice in every twenty-four-hour period the tide rose and fell, and when it was necessary to flood the fields—and it frequently was during the summer months—rice-trunk-docks, or gates, were raised and water came in on an incoming tide. Or, as the desire may be, when the gates were raised the water left the fields on an outgoing tide. Mr. Bondurant had been known to say that God had given him land with the perfect pitch of the tide and had made him wealthy. He was a religious man, and gave much of his wealth to Goose Creek Church, where he served as a warden.

To the right, near the river, was the large expanse of salt marsh that had been indicated on the map with tufts of grass. Tiny waterways meandered through the tall, green cordgrasses, and all sorts of wildlife lived in the salt marshes, including many shorebirds. It was here that Mr. Bondurant had taken his sons during night hours to view the changing underwater spectacle by the light of torches.

To the far right was an upland range of some height, and on the pinnacle stood the two circular towers of brick.

"See those towers?" Matt asked.

"Of course. How could anyone with two eyes not see them?"

Ignoring the crack, Matt said, "That is where the plantation workers found refuge during storms, as the rising water from the river and marsh would not reach the top of that hill. Do you know of a more perfect place for a sphinx?"

"No, but that doesn't mean that the statue is there. In fact, it is *not* there, for if it were, Father would have seen it many times."

"It *has* to be there," Matt reasoned. "From almost any point on this portion of the Cooper River a monument on that bluff would be noticeable."

"Of course that would be the perfect place, but perhaps the Spaniards did not choose to build it on the most logical spot," Josh said.

"They would build it there, and it is up to us to locate it."

"It's going to take some doing to get to that ridge," Josh observed. "We cannot walk through the marsh."

Matt surveyed the area. "True. We'll have to backtrack, and go through the forest and come in from the other side, and it's no short journey."

"Want to try it today?" Josh asked.

"Have you lost your senses? Of course we'll go today. If we're going to locate the sphinx in three days, we don't have a day to lose."

"You said it."

After a while they came upon a mound of earth on which jasmine vines bloomed in a blaze of yellow. "That's where the girl was buried standing up," Matt commented.

"A sad story," Josh said, skirting around the yellow flowers growing on a mound higher than his head. "Some of our ancestors went through difficult times."

"But none more so than the Bondurant who couldn't bear to think of his young daughter lying in the ground and had her buried in an upright position."

"The fevers took their toll on the Bondurants," Josh said.

"They took their toll on every planter family," Matt observed. "Something about the stagnant fields causes illness, but don't dwell on such horrible thoughts. We're wasting precious time." As they trudged through the woods, picking their way around trees, Spanish sword, and jumping ditches, Matt and Josh came to realize the magnitude of their search.

Finally, they came out of the woods and there before them, high on a bluff, stood the twin towers. Both Matt and Josh sucked in their breath.

Matt pushed back some prickly vines. "Follow me."

9

"WOW-EE!" JOSH LOOKED UP at the towers on top of what seemed like a mountain.

"The mound is so high," Matt said. "It's too high."

"What do you mean *too* high? It's as high as it is," Josh replied.

"It's as high as it is, but that mound of earth didn't start out being that high."

"Be specific. What are you getting at?" Josh sometimes became impatient with Matt, when Matt didn't fully explain something that was perfectly obvious to him.

"I mean that the mound is man-made. There is no way under heaven that a hill that high exists in this flat land called the Low Country."

"Who built it, if it's man-made?"

Matt thought for a few seconds, his mind going over every possibility he could think of. His eyes bored into the towers with the utmost concentration. He frowned and a puzzled expression settled on his face. Josh stared at his brother, mesmerized, and finally Matt spoke. "The people who built the towers also built the mound."

"Why would they build such a mound?"

"Can't you understand that? If they planned to construct towers where the plantation workers would be safe, they needed to build them on the highest elevation, but there was no high elevation on this property so they had to build one."

"Where did they get the dirt?" Josh asked.

Matt thought about the question, wondering, and suddenly the logical answer came to him. "Likely from the canals they dug in the rice fields."

From this place Josh could not view the rice fields, but he pictured them in his mind: large, flat fields, each with a series of canals that fed into the Cooper River. It made sense that the dirt taken from the canals would be somewhere, and there would be no better place to put it than in a mound on which they could build towers unreachable by rising tidal water. "I think you're right."

Matt looked around slowly. Although he and his brother had viewed the towers many times, they had never observed them from just this angle, and the towering brick shafts had taken on a new character. This was a baronial place, with its immense high hill, covered in the most luxuriant green and waxy foliage. The plant life must be at least two feet deep, he imagined. And somewhere in this tangled mass of greenery was a sphinx, he was sure of it. The thought of it shocked Matt so that he stood bolt upright and gripped his arms. He was shaking! Even in the most thrilling moments of his life, like when his parents had taken him and Josh on the Grand Tour of Europe, he had not shaken from the very bottom of his feet as he was now doing. As unsettled as he was, he admitted to himself that it was going to require some intensive pursuit and grinding labor to locate the sphinx. *Surely most Bondurants, being men of intelligence, have considered at some time or other that the sphinx would be somewhere on the mound?* he asked himself. But he felt no sense of helplessness or despair. *He* would find it.

"What are we going to do first?" Josh asked.

"Climb the hill and look around."

Observing Matt from behind as they pulled their way through tall, scraggly weeds and fought stiff, thorny ones, Josh thought, he is nervous. If only I can make him feel relaxed, at ease, we'll have a more pleasant time. And so he said, "Matt, I'm with you, boy. With you all the way. You can count on me."

Matt didn't answer, as his mind was on one thing: finding the sphinx.

"I'm sorry I doubted you," Josh added.

There was no response, and the twins pressed on until they reached the summit, with Matt arriving first and Josh wriggling up behind him, looking about curiously. "The hill didn't look this high from the first viewpoint," Josh observed.

Matt was still occupied with his own thoughts. "The towers are so tall. So amazingly tall."

"Are we going inside?" Josh asked.

Matt was still endeavoring to quell the anxiety flaring within him. He nodded his head to indicate yes, and when he found himself automatically walking toward an opening, his taut body relaxed a little.

Josh decided to leave Matt to his own thoughts and follow along.

Although the structure was of brick, the door had obviously been of marble, as three pieces of marble lay at the foot of the gaping doorway.

Matt stepped inside, gazing down and then up. Josh was behind him, also looking around.

Matt saw a blue sky through the top of the building. "There was once a roof of wood, but it has rotted away, except for a little around the edges."

"And the rain has come inside for hundreds of years," Josh said, kicking the silt under his feet.

Matt went to a wall and let his fingers slide over several bricks. "I can tell that once there were steps that led up to something, probably a platform where people stood while waiting for the storm to abate."

"Look!"

"What is it?" Matt asked. His voice echoed.

"It looks like the den of an animal," Josh said.

Matt went over to another part of the wall and kicked the dirt floor. "Whatever it is that enjoys lolling here must not mind getting wet."

Josh looked upward, then back at the door. "Whatever he is, he doesn't live here. There are no signs of an animal having eaten anything in the den, and it seems to me to be only a sleeping place."

Matt, again looking up, didn't respond, but allowed his wonderment to overtake him. "How round it is. Round and up, round and up."

"What do you say we take a look at the other tower?" Josh asked.

Matt started for the doorway. "The sun is moving across the sky, and we don't have all the time in the world."

No more than twenty feet from the first tower stood the other. Like the first, a gaping hole was the doorway, and pieces of marble lay on the ground. Inside it looked the same as the other building, except there was no place where an animal had dug out a den.

Josh looked up at the sky through the rotted-away roof. "Matt, do any people come here now? During a hurricane, I mean?"

"I don't think so," Matt responded. "We haven't had a really bad storm for several years, and much would have to be done to the towers to protect the people from rain."

Josh didn't answer, and after a few moments of deep contemplation, Matt said, "I'm going to start writing my journal about the sphinx when I get home, beginning with our first discoveries. Today, the twenty-fourth day of April, 1846, an account of a portion of the history of South Carolina will begin."

Sitting at the desk in the library, Matt's mind worked rapidly and with its usual shrewdness. He began the narrative of the search for the sphinx at the beginning.

> There are moments of my early life that have been lost in the quicksand of time, sinking beneath the surface and leaving not a ripple to indicate their presence. But my search for the sphinx will not be lost in the depths of loose sand. Not only is every

twinkling instant of it etched on my mind, but even the most obvious and uninspiring events shall be recorded here. This journal, this narrative, is my heart and my breath.

April 24, 1846

The sculptures on the hill are two brick towers, like overseers watching the sparkling Cooper River, which is the heart of the entire plantation, all of it. That muscular organ, by rhythmic tidal contractions and relaxations, keeps all in motion. It is the center of the total personality of The Bond, imparting spirit, courage, and enthusiasm. A sudden inability of the river to function would ruin The Bond. There would be no rice crop, and no revenue. After a time there would be no helpers, no implements, and no pride. But the river, thanks be to God, experiences no sorrow, and it continues to be compassionate and merciful, circulating throughout the center of this estate. From it, we are who we are, and what we are, and it has ever been so.

Today the region of the Cooper River seized the attentions of my brother Josh and myself and turned them away from Hell Hole Swamp, a place where atrocious crimes have been committed, and probably shall be again. But our fears of that place were stilled by the expectation of discovery, and what a discovery we made! We found nature's treasure trove, the gem in the crown of animalic phenomena: a giant reptile that should only figure in a fantastical tale. It is unreal and yet it is there, dispelling all our beliefs. Our attentions could only be redirected by the enthrallment of another plantation presence. Look! There shows on a map of another era a sphinx somewhere near the river. I know that it is there, and I intend to expose it to the world.

Today my brother and I went to the brick towers, built more than a century ago for the protection of slaves during hurricanes. We didn't find the remotest indication of the sphinx, but I know that it is there. Perhaps tomorrow will be the day we shall make that discovery.

My brother is physically stronger than I, and he thinks that I have a stronger mental ability than he. Who is to say? We are different, close, serene, scrappy, honest, Bondurants. Neither my brother nor I desire to study at Cambridge, but we shall leave soon for that honored institution. Before we sail, we shall find the sphinx.

10

BACK AT THE TOWERS the next day, Josh and Matt began to look for clues that might give them a glimpse into the secret life of the tall structures. Signs of neglect were reminders that the field hands hadn't been evacuated from their houses during a hurricane for many years.

Hurricanes came in clusters, it seemed, almost in ten-year terms of assault, and for the past years, since 1822 according to Mr. Bondurant, there hadn't been one that washed away whole families and destroyed rice fields. To lose the low-lying fields would be almost as devastating as losing a member of the family, for an entire year's work would be washed away, and many people would suffer from a lack of funds and food.

But today the sun was shining hard on the towers as well as on the recently planted rice fields, which extended away from the towers in several directions. Josh and Matt occasionally stopped their search long enough to gaze across the scene that was half-land and half-water. Very soon now, the seed would sprout, and little green shoots would be covered in river water, which would wash away insects that devoured the tender shoots. After the flow of water had remained on the sprouts long enough to wash away the insects, the fields would be drained, and the plants would grow and prosper in the long days of southern sunshine that brought on further growth. But as insects swarmed in to attack the fragile plants, there would be another "flow," when the vast fields would again be covered in water, coming into the canals on a high tide.

The fields took on certain seasons. Seedtime was the beginning, and then came the germinal period. The greening was next, and it wasn't uncommon to see people standing on bluffs, allowing the ocean of greenery to boost their spirits. And after the ripening came the harvest, the autumnal equinox. One year's rice production, from seedtime to harvest, was a lifetime, four definite, rhythmic periods of the pilgrimage. Only those who lived it were to know it.

There were, of course, events and traumas that stalled the journey, such as disease, war, and hurricane, and there were reminders of each, including the twin towers.

While Matt carefully examined the inside wall of a tower, Josh consulted the dirt floor, kicking and smoothing the silt with his feet.

"There was only one door," Matt remarked. "The people who came here for shelter entered through the door, remained for the duration of the storm, and left by the the same opening."

Josh gazed around. "It must have been stifling here during bad weather."

"Stifling, yes. Tall and high, but confined and cramped. It was horrid, I am sure."

"Hey! I thought an animal had been sleeping here, but I didn't notice *this* before!" Josh said, on his knees examining the sandy soil. "There's no hair in the dirt."

Matt stopped gazing up and turned toward his twin. "Strange. Unless the animal has no hair."

"What kind of creature would that be, Brain?"

"It wouldn't be an alligator, that's for sure. Not this far from the water. But an alligator doesn't have any hair."

"The den's big," Josh said as he picked up a handful of dirt and let it sprinkle through his fingers to the floor. "Whatever snoozes here is huge," he added as he smelled the dirt left in his hand. "There's no odor." He shook his head and rubbed his hands on his britches. "No clues. The only way we can discover what kind of animal comes here is to surprise it with a visit."

"You think you're up to that?" Matt asked, his eyes wide as he envisioned his brother facing a strange animal.

Thinking back on a huge black bear that had ambled up to the house one day, and the time a wild boar came from the woods, digging its ivory tusks in the sand, Josh answered, "Not really. Let's go outside. It's clear the sphinx isn't in the towers."

"How could the sphinx be in the towers?" Matt asked, shaking his head at such a stupid remark. "The sphinx is as big as the granary, or even larger, and how do you think that could fit into one of these cylindrical buildings?"

"Then where would it fit, Your Brilliance?" Josh shot back. "Of course it wouldn't fit in the towers, but *where* is it?"

"That's for us to find out."

Matt and Josh stood on the hill and gazed at the tangled growth of maybe a hundred years that covered the ground. "It's bewildering," Matt said, finally. "We know from the map that the sphinx *was* somewhere around here. It actually existed, and I don't believe it would have vanished in the salt air."

"Then what do you think happened to it?"

For a long time Matt didn't answer, and Josh stood by him indulgently, his hands in his pockets. Then Matt said, "If there was an easy answer, someone else would have found the statue. Because the discovery will be a difficult one, no person up to now has had the diligence, the determination to be successful. But we are at least a little above the ordinary, do you not think so, Twin?"

"If we ever find it we'll be above the ordinary. There's no question about that. But are we truly intelligent enough to figure it out? Surely Father knows more than we know, and he hasn't found it."

"Goofy! Father never found the sphinx, but that doesn't rule anything out," Matt answered, playfully kicking his brother in the leg. "Not only *could* we find the sphinx, but we *will* find it."

Josh went down the hill, half-walking, half-sliding, as he held onto weeds to keep from falling and rolling down to the bottom. Matt was coming behind, more slowly, and when he reached his brother, Josh was already walking away, his hands in his pockets and his head down.

"What's wrong now?" Matt demanded. "You look about ready to be laid away in the family plot at Goose Creek Church."

Josh didn't turn toward his brother. "There's no way under the sun we can find the sphinx," he muttered. "And that's if it exists at all, which I am not sure that it does."

Matt stopped and gave a last look up at the towers, not allowing himself to be swayed by Josh's words enough to acknowledge that what he said could be true. Finally, his gaze circled toward a grove of oaks and pines, back of the rice fields, a place that he and Josh rarely visited but a spot where a sphinx might be located. However, time would be involved in such a search, he was thinking, and he was in no mood to be rushed by his twin, whose only desire was to go back to Hell Hole Swamp. He ran and caught up with Josh. "You just cannot wait to go back to the swamp, can you?"

Josh didn't answer, and finally Matt said, "All right. Let's go home for today, but we'll go slowly and give the woods a careful look."

Josh, happy that Matt seemed to be giving up for that day, replied, "Agreed. Lead on." He followed his brother, whose eyes were taking in huge roots that jutted out, as well as fallen trees, Spanish sword, pine needles, and other debris.

"Look, Twin," Josh yelled, "I see something." His eyes were wide.

By the time Matt ran over, Josh was on his knees, poking in the dirt beside a fallen limb that was covered in Spanish moss. He lifted the limb, jerking the moss which had stuck to the ground. "As sure's my name's Joshua Bondurant, we've found something."

Matt, unable to suppress his enthusiasm, grabbed the stick from Josh's hand and broke it over a knee.

"Just who do you think you are?" Josh questioned.

"I'm Matthew Bondurant, one-half of the team that found the sphinx on The Bond plantation."

Josh let it go. Never in his life had he seen Matt so excited.

Matt was now using the stick to dig away dirt, and Josh joined him, digging with his hands.

"Matt, whatever this object is, it's made of tabby. It really *is* tabby."

Matt jumped up, threw his arms toward the sky, and yelled, "By Uncle Tidyman's mustache, we've found the sphinx!"

Josh didn't answer, as he was digging so fast that his heart was beating in his throat. Finally he stood up, took a deep breath, and rubbed his hands on his britches. His fingernails were packed with soil. Taking another breath, he said, "If this *is* the sphinx, no person in the world can take away from us the credit for finding it, but how did Uncle Tidyman get into this? We haven't seen him in over two years."

Matt, ignoring the remark and not taking his eyes from the object, commented, "This part of the statue is round."

Josh fell back to his knees, and using his fingers like a hoe, raked back handfuls of dirt. Stopping for a moment to catch his breath, he glanced at the exposed object. "It's a toe."

"A toe! Are you sure?"

"I'm sure. Look at the toenail."

"It *is* a toe!" Matt jumped up and down and screamed, "We've found the foot of the sphinx!"

"Don't be too sure," Josh warned.

"What's wrong with you? Surely you don't think that round object with a nail is anything but a toe."

"It's a toe all right, but it's too small for a toe on the foot of the sphinx."

Matt thought about that, and his heart sank. "Maybe the sphinx wasn't as large as suspected," he rationalized.

Josh went on digging until he had exposed another toe. "This *can't* be the sphinx."

"It's a grave marker," Matt said, coming closer than ever before to using profanity, but he quickly reminded himself that no provocation would make him resort to that. His father had told him that there were far too many beautiful words in the English language to use to express oneself without using profanity. But as he thought about his disappointment, Matt finally growled, "It's only a blankety-blank, capital blankety-blank grave marker." Feeling as weak and useless as the residue left on the seabeach after the tide had gone out, he pushed himself to help Josh scrape away dirt until they could see a portion of a flat grave marker made of tabby. It was inscribed: *Abraham. May he rest in peace.*

The twins stood up, their posture slouched. "I would have bet my life that we'd found the sphinx," Matt said. "And we only discovered an old burial ground."

"That's something," Josh pointed out. "Father will be pleased to know that it's here, and he'll have it cleaned and preserved."

"You're an incurable optimist," Matt answered, as they left for home. That night Matt wrote in his journal:

> April 25, 1846
>
> Today my brother Joshua and I discovered a tabby claw in the forest, and we believed it to be a part of the sphinx. But fortune did not befriend us. It was only a burial marker. We will not give up the search, even though the day after tomorrow we go back to our original project—trying to rescue the baby raccoon from the three-fingered hands of the giant lizard.

11

"I'M GOING BACK to Hell Hole Swamp with you but only because I promised," Matt grumbled on the fourth day after the failed search. "Don't allow the thought to enter your head that I've given up the search for the sphinx."

Josh ran to a tree by the side of the road, pulled himself up to a limb until his chin was above it, and slowly let himself down. Making a face to downplay this achievement, he said, "Leave off your worrying. We'll find it."

"I said you are an incurable optimist," Matt answered, running ahead to the next limb to try to "chin" it—and failing. Waving a hand toward the tree as though dismissing the stunt as too trivial, he said, "Wish I were as positive as you."

"You are. You're my twin and we're alike."

Now entering the dark and gloomy road The Shadows, talk turned to the lizard.

"Do you think he'll be here?" Josh asked.

"How would I know? *I* don't think like a lizard, but if the lizard thinks as *I* do, he's gone."

"Down-in-the-mouth Matthew," Josh ridiculed. "He'll be here and I'm going to rescue the raccoon from those three-fingered hands. That's my goal, just as yours is finding the sphinx."

"I'll be watching," Matt said.

Just then they came to the pool, and the lizard was nowhere in sight.

"He's a boy, and he's playing a game with us," Josh stated, his hands on his hips.

"What makes you think he's a boy? Looks more like a man to me."

"He just looks and acts like a boy, even though he's big enough to be a man," Josh reasoned.

"He probably *is* a boy. If he'd been a man he'd have eaten us by now."

Josh grabbed a tree limb above his head and made his way across the inlet. When he dropped to the ground his feet didn't catch traction, and they slid right out from under him. The next thing he knew, he was in a ditch, immediately beside a large snake that was coiled about three times. Its neck was extended and its tongue was darting out and in, out and in. In a flash the fangs struck Josh on the leg just under the knee.

"*Help!* I've been bitten by a snake."

Matt flew as fast as he could over the inlet. When he dropped down beside Josh, he could see the snake slithering under a clump of water lily leaves. Although Matt and Josh needled each other constantly, Matt instinctively knew that his brother was in trouble and it was up to him to save his life. Somewhere in his brain a thought stirred, reminding Matt that when a person was bitten by a snake, it helped if one could fetch the reptile for identification. It must quickly be determined if the snake was of a poisonous species and whether or not it had expelled all of its venom. Of course if the reptile had rattles on its tail, that would be a clue that it was a rattlesnake, a dangerous variety.

"Get back, Josh," Matt screamed. "I'm going for the snake."

"Don't do it, Matt. It'll get you, too."

"I don't care. I've got to get him." Matt picked up a limb, raked back the leaves, and there before his eyes the snake was coiled, its neck extended and the tongue darting out and in. Matt struck the reptile until he was quite sure

it was dead, and he slid the stick under the shining skin and lifted it up. Rattles were plainly visible.

Although Josh was feeling no pain, he wanted to get home in a flash, and as he and Matt, holding the stick high with the dead snake dangling from it, flew along The Shadows, he asked, "Do you think I'll die?"

"No. There's treatment for snakebite," Matt explained. "An old slave named Caesar got his freedom for perfecting such a treatment. Father has the record of Caesar's release from bondage, as well as the antidote for the poison. But we have to get you home, and *now*!"

"Where will we say we were?" Josh asked as they passed the Lydia Oak. "I don't want to reveal anything about the lizard and Hell Hole Swamp."

"Just say in the woods," Matt advised. "Believe me, our parents will be so frightened they'll never question anything as unimportant as that."

12

Mr. Bondurant was standing on the pillared veranda of the mansion, looking across the lawns toward the woods. As far as the eye could see in any direction, the land was his, having come down to him from his father, who had inherited the place from his father, another Bondurant. It was a place to be proud of, and Mr. Bondurant knew that he was fortunate to have been born here, at The Bond, a plantation that bore a part of his name.

Just then he saw two figures hurrying toward the mansion. One of them was carrying something hanging over a stick. As they got closer he recognized them as Joshua Matthew, but what was Matthew carrying on the stick? he wondered.

Squinting into the sun, he could see them better now, and although they were not running, they certainly were hurrying along, and he believed that something was wrong. Usually they meandered at a slower pace, and they rarely made their way straight for the house, coming across the lawn. Mr. Bondurant started toward them, and then paused on the steps. Matthew was carrying a dead snake on the stick, and he was pointing toward Joshua's leg. *Joshua had been bitten by the snake!*

"Caleb!" Mr. Bondurant screamed to a servant in the distance. The man turned briefly, then started running toward the house.

Mr. Bondurant was fairly sure that Josh had been bitten by the snake, as his sons frequently encountered reptiles on the plantation, but they never brought them home after they had killed them. And the countenance on their faces, which he could now detect, was grim.

"Caleb," Mr. Bondurant called out before the man had reached the steps, "go at once and fetch Dr. Horry from Mepkin Plantation. Tell him that I believe one of my sons has suffered snakebite."

"Yes, Cap'n," Caleb said, breaking into a run for the stables, where he would get a horse on which to ride to the plantation, several miles away.

Mrs. Bondurant, sensing something had happened, came to the door and immediately comprehended the situation. "Have you sent for Dr. Horry?"

"Yes," her husband answered.

Wringing her hands distractedly, she added, "Do you not think we should rely on Caesar's antidote while we wait? Suppose Dr. Horry is not at home?"

"You are quite right," her husband answered. "I'll go to the library and try to locate it. Pray that I can find it quickly."

"I felt the snake puncture my leg just below the knee," Josh called to his mother, "but I'm feeling no pain. Perhaps the snake didn't expel all of its venom."

"Just the same," she said calmly, concealing the fear that had filled her entire body, "come upstairs. You must go to bed, and lie still until Caleb returns with Dr. Horry."

"Where is Father?" Matt asked, lowering the dead reptile to the steps.

"He is in the library, searching for Caesar's antidote."

"Is that the remedy concocted by a slave who won his freedom for the medicine?" Matt queried, stepping inside the house.

"Yes. There is a copy in the library, and if your father can find it, we shall begin administering the antidote immediately."

Several servants had gathered in the entrance hall, and Mr. Bondurant pushed through and came to Joshua. "I have found Caesar's remedy, but before we begin with it, I must see the snake."

"It's on the steps, Father," Matthew said, leading the way as his father followed him outside.

Mrs. Bondurant and Josh went upstairs, where a servant had folded back the sheet and counterpane and plumped up the pillows. Josh removed his trousers and climbed into bed.

Mrs. Bondurant explained to Josh that Dr. Horry had studied medicine at the College of Charleston and would know what to do for snakebite, but in the meantime the remedy perfected by Caesar would be started, just in case Dr. Horry would be away on another sick call.

Josh told his mother just what had happened, but he was careful not to say where he and Matt were when the accident occurred. Just as Matt had predicted, their mother was so concerned over her son's health she didn't question where he had encountered the snake. After the conversation, Josh moved slightly, and asked for something for pain.

"All right," Mrs. Bondurant said as she left quickly, and within minutes a servant carried in a tray with a demijohn of old wine and a glass. The glass was filled and handed to Josh, who raised up and held the glass to his lips with both hands.

"*Stop!*" Mr. Bondurant screamed as he stepped into the room and then bolted toward Josh. He knocked the glass from Josh's hands, and red wine splashed out and stained the white counterpane.

"What in the world?" Mrs. Bondurant questioned, her eyes wide.

"Father! Are you insane?" Matt asked. For a boy who usually cajoled his brother, he was intense and worried.

"No. I have not lost my senses." Mr. Bondurant ran his hands through his hair. His face was distraught and pale, and he licked his dry lips. "But that wine would slow the heartbeat, and the snake's venom also slows the heart. I'm not sure Joshua's body could accommodate both dosages. The snake was a rattler."

"Was all the venom expelled?" Josh queried.

"I don't know, son," his father answered. "Dr. Horry will take the rattlesnake to the carpenter shop and dissect it for that determination."

"Let me take a look at your leg, Joshua," Mrs. Bondurant said, lifting the sheet.

Josh flipped both legs from underneath the covering, and it was clear the left one was swollen.

"Oh, my goodness," Mrs. Bondurant wailed.

"Bear up, now," Josh's father said, taking Josh's foot in his hand. "Do you know where the fangs struck?"

"Just under my knee, on the side."

"Look," Mr. Bondurant remarked somberly. "There is the puncture."

"I can see them clearly," Mrs. Bondurant said, "near the ankle."

"My Lord," her husband cried, visibly shaken. "You are right. There were two strikes near the ankle, but I was looking at the one under the knee."

"How many punctures are there, Father?" Matt asked.

"I don't know, but it's clear Joshua was bitten several times, and it's likely the snake expelled all of its venom."

"Have you found the antidote?" Mrs. Bondurant asked.

"Yes." He went outside in the hall and picked up the scroll he had put on the table when he noticed that Josh was about to drink the old wine. "Please come in and help us," he said to two servants in the hallway.

Mrs. Bondurant hurriedly cleared a table and lighted a lamp. "Put it here so you can see it clearly."

Her husband unrolled the paper from both ends and began to read from script written with flourishes and large, curling Ss. The document was dated, *In the year of our Lord 1749 to the 31st day of May 1750.* Mr. Bondurant's voice was low and determined as he read:

> The said gentleman accordingly withdrew. And being returned Capt. Taylor reported to the House that he had pursuant to their order delivered the message which they had in charge to the governor. And that his excellency had desired them to acquaint

> this House that he would send an answer by a messenger of his own.

Mr. Bondurant looked away from the scroll and explained to his family, "These people were members of the House of Representatives, and they obviously are discussing the question of the slave's cure for rattlesnake bite, and ultimately his freedom for perfecting it." He read on:

> Mr. Irving reported from the Committee who were appointed to inquire into the cures said to be performed by the Negro Caesar by an antidote against poison, and to procure from him a discovery of the said antidote.

"Hurry! Hurry!" Mrs. Bondurant urged her husband. "Get to the formula so that we can mix it for Joshua."

Mr. Bondurant's eyes scanned the scroll and he skipped over a large amount of writing. Finally, he read:

> That the Committee have pursuant to the order of the House examined into the cases performed by the said Negro Caesar and the efficiency of his antidote for expelling of poison and it appeared to the Committee that the said Caesar had cured several persons who had been long ill of a lingering intolerable pain in the stomach and bowels, particularly Mrs. John Cattall, Mr. Henry Middleton, and Mrs. Galliard, who had employed some of the most skillful physicians in this country and found no relief from their medicines. The Committee finding Caesar had no opportunity of making tryal of any experiments upon animals, they insisted upon his discovery every thing he knew concerning the fever of poisons, together with the names of the plants which he made use of performing the aforesaid cures, and his method of preparing the same, as likewise the symptoms by which he knew when any person was poisoned, which he said he would faithfully comply with and...

"Go on. For goodness sake get to the ingredients," Mrs. Bondurant pleaded.

"I'm coming to it right now."

Mrs. Bondurant turned to the servants. "When you know what the ingredients for this formula are, go at once and bring them here."

"Father, can you please give me something for pain?" Josh begged.

Both parents and Matt came to the bed. Mrs. Bondurant let up a stifled scream when she looked at her son's leg, which no longer resembled a leg, but a rectangular box, with only the slightest wavy place at the end. That is where Josh's toes were.

"Son, I cannot give you anything to reduce the pain. It is just too dangerous."

Matt held a pillow close to his brother's arm. "Hit this pillow as hard as you can and picture yourself smacking that snake. Maybe that will take away the edge of pain."

"Nothing will take it away," Josh said, trying his best to hold back tears.

Mr. Bondurant hurried back to the lamp and read:

> The cure for poison: Take the roots of plantain and wild horehound, dried or fresh, boil them together and two quarts of water to one quart and strain it. Of this concoction let the patient take one third part three mornings, fasting, from which if he finds no relief after the third day, it is a sign that the patient had not been poisoned at all.
>
> The plantain or horehound will either of them cure alone, but they are more efficient together. In summer you may take one handful of the roots of goldenrod compounded with rum and lye, together with an application of tobacco leaves soaked in rum in case of rattlesnake bite.

"Go to the garden and bring roots of plantain," Mrs. Bondurant instructed the servants. "And fetch wild horehound from the pantry."

Within the hour Josh was given his first dose of Caesar's cure, and when the physician arrived at the house, his only prescription in addition to that remedy was cold compresses to the foot and leg to bring down the swelling. The physician went to the carpenter shop, where the dead snake had been taken, and when he returned he announced that it had expelled all of its venom.

The doctor remained at the mansion, and when night came, he sat on a chair just outside the bedroom door. Mr. and Mrs. Bondurant and Matt also remained in the hallway, and servants passed into and out of the room, carrying large porcelain bowls of cool artesian water. Cloths were dipped into the water and placed on Josh's leg and foot. The night stretched out long and weary, and Josh believed he had never known such agony.

After three days the pain abated. Josh lay quietly in bed, which was not to his liking, but he did much thinking during the quiet hours. Time after time he pictured the raccoon in the hand of the giant lizard at Hell Hole Swamp. Although he had tried his best to free the animal, he had not been successful, and besides that, the twins had been unable to locate the sphinx. Every day that passed was a day closer to the time when they would leave the plantation for England, and as he thought about that, it came to Josh that when he and Matt returned from England, nothing would ever be quite the same again. They would be older, and have interests in subjects that now they knew nothing about. Life was changing, just as surely as the sand was different after each ebb and flow of the tides.

Of course there was another way to look at things. The two greatest discoveries that would likely ever be made at The Bond were still open to them, if only they could be successful. To identify the species of lizard while freeing the raccoon and to find the sphinx would be achievements that would glow as brightly as any star in the galaxy of plantation achievements, but the goals seemed out of reach.

13

"AN OLD CEMETERY?" Mr. Bondurant walked over to a window and gazed out at the lawn. It was the middle of May. Technically, summer was yet to arrive, but Mother Nature did not hold to man's calendar. Azaleas had shed their color and sprouted new, greener leaves. "I'll send some workers there tomorrow to do some excavating and a cleanup."

"May I help?" Matt asked. "While in that region of the plantation I can keep an eye toward any sign of the sphinx."

Mr. Bondurant made for the door, and was striding with that certain dignity that was so much a part of his character when he turned, and with his voice lower said, "The discovery of the sphinx would give us added prominence. I wish you Godspeed."

The twins watched the tall, ramrod-straight figure go into the hallway and disappear down the stairs.

"Josh, I'm going to help with the cleanup, and I'll keep an eye out for the sphinx." Matt studied his fingernails for a moment, thinking, then added, "While you're here in bed, you can help me."

"Is your head in a deep well? How can *I* help, flat in bed and helpless?"

"There *must* be a clue that'll help us find the sphinx."

"What sort of clue?" Josh asked.

"I'd wager there's an answer that's fairly obvious, and someday, when we know precisely where the sphinx is located, we'll think we were pretty dumb not to notice it."

"You're either blind or daft," Josh answered, his head almost buried in the thick, soft pillows, and the bedclothes thrown back from his body. The last two weeks had been torture, and another week of confinement stretched before him. Right at that moment Josh was thinking how fortunate Matt was to be able to move about and go anywhere on the plantation he desired. As he thought about it, all the people he could envision, as they were going about their daily duties, were in a way detached from him, abstract, and *his* whole world went no farther than the sides of the bed. He rose up on an elbow, then lay back on the pillows and wiped his face with the back of his hand.

"You feeling all right?" Matt asked.

"The weather's getting warmer daily, and it'd drive anybody bloody mad to stay in this bed as I'm having to do."

"You could look on it as an opportunity."

"Opportunity?"

"Absolutely. I'm going to the library and bring a novel for you to read. The story is about an Egyptian princess, and there's a lot in it about the sphinx near Cairo, Egypt. Your last week in bed won't be wasted, as you're going to discover the clue that'll lead us to our sphinx."

Matt brought the book, which had an illustration of an Egyptian princess on the cover. Josh eyed the beautiful woman for a second, then let the pages fall aside in his hands. There were many drawings of sphinxes, and a seed of hope sprouted in his mind. If he had to remain in bed another week, perhaps he *would* enjoy reading this book, and if Matt was right, and there could be a sort of clue that would help them find the sphinx, the week would not be wasted. Finally, he turned to his brother. "I'll read the book and search for a clue, but only if you make me a solemn promise."

Matt got up and grandly bowed from the waist. "And what is it my honorable twin desires?"

"One week from today," Josh said, ignoring the dramatic display, "the first day I'm released from this prison of a bed, we go to Hell Hole Swamp. I haven't given up on freeing the raccoon, you know."

"That raccoon's probably half-grown now," Matt protested. "And more than likely back with its family."

"That has nothing to do with what I said. *The first day I'm back on my feet we go to Hell Hole Swamp*!"

Matt waved a hand. "Agreed."

"The giant lizard is just as important a discovery as any sphinx. You just won't admit it."

"It *is* important. We have two major discoveries, and we can solve both mysteries if we keep our heads attached to our bodies."

Josh looked at Matt's face and recognized that under the countenance was a determination that wouldn't relent until he had found the sphinx. Matt was driven, a mite hungry even, to locate the tabby statue, and he would know no peace until the job was done, Josh believed. A tight smile on his face after Matt left gave the impression that Josh was just as dedicated, but his interest was in the lizard and raccoon. The twins were the same in the flesh, but inside they had different aspirations and when Josh finally opened the book it was as though in protest.

Within minutes he was enchanted with the story and his eyes shone as he read about a city near the Nile River, which silvered in the moonlight, the same as South Carolina's Cooper River. He read on and out of the pages emerged images of those who exulted in life centuries ago. But Josh didn't indulge in flights of fantasy, as his intention was to find the clue to the location of the sphinx, if indeed such a clue was in the book.

As he turned the pages, details of Egypt etched themselves on his mind. The mummies and how they had been preserved were a curiosity. Drawings revealed open lids of caskets, and the glitter of glass eyes. Lips of both men and women were rouged, and they wore wigs. Sometimes a king's ransom in precious stones was buried with a monarch, and grave robbers in search of the jewels had ransacked handsome sarcophagi. Josh wiggled his nose as he read of the fragrance of ancient spices that filled the air when robbers lifted a glass cover. How different were Egyptian tombs from plantation burial sites, but there *was* one similarity, Josh believed. People from South Carolina revered their ancestors, even though they didn't have the complicated and massive family trees of Egyptian dynasties. As he thought about it, there were other likenesses, such as the ibis, the sacred bird of Egypt. Flocks of them lived among South Carolina waterways. Were they descendants of the ibises from the Nile?

Now permitting himself to take a flight of fantasy, Josh pushed aside the book and let his mind explore the goddesses, kings, queens, and pharaohs, and how all of those people invariably wished for an easy death and a goodly burial. He'd never thought about *his* death and burial. That was something that would come about naturally, as it had with all of the Bondurant ancestors. But Egyptians of wealth prepared their tombs and obituaries well in advance of the ends of their lives, and rulers, while at the peak of glory in the prime of their reign, worked constantly on their burial plans. Wealth was no limit to them, and they were people with enormous energies, love of beauty, and unlimited labor sources. Their tombs were the most dramatic of all their statuary, and more notice was taken of the monuments than of the remains of the people who lay under them.

Kingdom rulers lay under the pyramids that crisscrossed the desert, and the largest of the pyramids were at Giza, a city on the Nile. The Great Pyramid, known as the Pyramid of Cheops, was the burial site of King Khufu, second king of the Fourth Dynasty, who became known to the Greeks as Cheops, and it loomed above the sphinx. *Egypt.* What a country!

Suddenly Josh pictured himself standing between the stone paws of the sphinx at Giza, and he was looking up at the mysterious gaze of the face. In his mind, as he looked, he was searching for a clue and was in deep concentration. It wasn't in the face, at least he didn't see a clue there now. Could there be one in the paws? Had the grave marker recently found been casually patterned after the sphinx? There were many sphinxes, and some of them even had the face of a woman, but as far as he could determine, they were in crouching shape and had paws. Could that be a clue?

Josh's thoughts went back to the faces of the sphinxes, especially the eyes. They were always searching, surveying a vanished city or a river delta. Was a clue to be found in the eyes? Had some former owner of the plantation seen himself as the Egyptians saw themselves, and had the planter constructed a sphinx as his tomb? If that was truly what had happened, the planter would surely have chosen tabby for his tomb, for it was the only masonry building material available on the coast of South Carolina.

If there was such a sphinx on the plantation, was there a sepulchre where a body had once been laid to rest? Was it a great cavern today? Could a sphinx have been as important a part of the Cooper River as the Egyptian tombs were to the Nile? The Cooper River was no Nile, he decided, but then Josh thought about it more carefully.

Just as the Nile had played an important part in Egyptian history, the Cooper River was the central force of The Bond, and other plantations as well. Without it there would be no waterway, no boat traffic, no avenue by which to transport rice to the Charleston market. Water journeys were one of the most important parts of each day on the plantation. There *could* be a correlation between the rivers, and just as the Egyptians had created sphinxes and other monuments to people known for their achievements, the planters, in a new land of prosperity, could have done the same.

After supper that night, Josh again read the book on Egypt, and he didn't put it aside until his eyes were heavy with fatigue. Egypt was truly fascinating, and the book was going to turn long, dreary days into short, exciting ones, he thought as he turned down the lamp. His conclusion was on the mark, and the last of Josh's period in bed flew by as if on the wings of ospreys. The night before Josh and Matt were to go to Hell Hole Swamp and try to renew acquaintance with the lizard, Josh thanked his twin brother for bringing him the book on Egypt.

"Did you read it carefully?" Matt asked.

"I believe I made a genuine acquaintance with Egypt."

"Making an acquaintance with Egypt wasn't the point of the research," Matt snapped. "I'd hoped you would find a clue to help us locate the sphinx."

"Perhaps I did."

"Josh! What are you saying? Did you find a cluc to the location of our tabby monument?"

Josh yawned. "I'm going to sleep," he mumbled with his mouth half-open.

Matt hit a knee with his fist. "Drat! *Did you find a clue?*"

Josh turned his back to his brother, and said on another yawn, "I've no intention of telling you the clue until we go back to Hell Hole Swamp and find the lizard and raccoon."

"You didn't discover a clue," Matt snarled. "You're being tricky. I don't believe you."

"Believe it or not," Josh retorted. "But I found a clue. The builder of the sphinx knew precisely where to situate it, and it's so obvious I cannot believe others haven't located it."

14

"ALL WEEK WHILE YOU LOLLED in bed and read of the wonders of ancient Egypt, *I* worked," Matt said, as he strolled next to his brother on the way to Hell Hole Swamp.

"*You* worked? That's inconceivable!"

Matt ignored his brother's catty remark. "I helped clean the cemetery and build the wood fence that encircles it. A gate is being cast."

"What's the design of the gate?"

Matt shook his head. "Only Father and the Good Lord know. You know how Father is about the ironworks on this plantation."

"So what's wrong with the way he is?"

"Nothing's wrong, Bonehead, and don't be so touchy. I suppose if Father wants to have the ironsmith execute an extraordinary design, cast it once, then destroy it so it cannot be copied, we'll always have original and unusual ironwork."

"Is the work on the cemetery completed?" Josh wanted to know.

"Down to the last pine needle," Matt answered. "I worked hard."

"Sure you did physical work, or are you trying to mislead me?"

Matt stopped walking and concentrated on his brother. "How about you? You sure *you* did something brainy, like study Egypt? If you're being honest, then you've changed."

Josh thought about that. "We did change roles for a few days, and I never believed such a thing could happen. It's a minor miracle."

"Not entirely. I didn't change roles with you, for I could never in the whole world withhold information from you about a clue to the location of the sphinx. Especially since we're in this together."

"You're fishing for the clue, but I won't tell," Josh said, firmly.

"Call it fishing if you want. I call it being adult."

"If you're so adult, then you must be casting glances at the ladies," Josh needled his brother, trying to get him off the subject of the clue.

"I admit I've looked at a couple. And what about you?"

"None in particular. Which one of the ladies have you honored with your dreamy gaze and poetic thoughts?"

"Why should I tell you? You're the one who enjoys holding out on information. I can do the same."

"Have it your way," Josh answered. "But I've noticed at church that you look over the hymnbook at Margaret Wigfall."

Matt flushed red and hastened around the bend in The Shadows until the swamp came into view.

"Do you see anything?" Josh asked, willing to drop the subject that so embarrassed his brother.

"Not yet."

"Let's go," Josh said, grabbing a limb and swinging his body across the first finger of murky water. When he dropped down on the marsh mud, he noticed two unsavory characters who were sitting on roots, beyond the next inlet.

"Wha' that?" a man asked.

"Nuthin'. You hearin' noises?"

"Who are those men?" asked Matt, just as he joined Josh.

"Hush! Don't you remember what Father said?"

"He said gangsters and people of no natural integrity come to this place," Matt whispered.

"Didn't he remind us that some people had been murdered here and their bodies were found in the pool?" Josh mouthed.

"Yes."

"I think we'd better leave, and right this minute."

"Wait. Let's see if we can tell what they're saying."

The twins stood as still as they could, almost holding their breath as they listened.

"Now you remember," a man whose face was smudged with dirt said, "that I have the barn key." He held up a key to a shaft of sunlight.

"Matt! Did you hear that?"

"Yes. He has a key to Father's barn. What do you think he plans to do with it?"

"How would I know?"

"Listen."

"And what good does that do you?" the other man asked. It was obvious that under the dirt the men were of fair skin, but their faces and clothes looked as though they had never seen soap and water.

"It'll do both of us plenty of good when the rice is in."

"How so?"

"You know that good, long-grain rice the cap'n keeps in them barrels in the barn? That rice he feeds his family with?"

The other man nodded.

"When that rice is in the barn, in the middle of the night I'll unlock the door, and we'll move them barrels down to the river and take 'em to Chars'n and we sell that rice for a big price."

The other man leaned back and roared with laughter. "Hey, where you get that barn key?"

"The man who keeps the barn, he likes the bottle."

"And you swapped him a bottle of whiskey for the barn key?"

Both men were leaning over, laughing gustily.

"Just wait until I tell Father," Josh hissed through clenched teeth.

"You cannot tell Father," Matt reminded his brother. "Where are you going to say you saw the men?"

"Matt, we *have* to tell Father. Those men'll steal all the rice from the barn. But if we tell Father, he'll punish us for coming to Hell Hole Swamp. He'll never permit us to come back here and I'll never again see the lizard."

"We'll have to see that these men are stopped," Matt concluded. "And that's another thing we cannot tell. It makes two: we cannot tell that we discovered the lizard and we must never mention that we came upon two gangsters."

"Snakes alive!" Josh said. "Hell Hole Swamp is full of secrets."

"Don't worry. When we find the sphinx, we'll tell everybody. The whole world will know."

"Get your mind off the sphinx and back on these people who're going to rob Father," Josh reprimanded. "You know we eat a bowl of rice every day, and think what it'll be like when it has been stolen. I've got to figure out a way to stop these men."

"And how do you propose to do that?" Matt asked.

"Shhh. Listen."

One of the men was standing up and stretching, and his clothes looked as if they were about to fall away from the thin frame. "That rice'll bring a high price in Chars'n."

"We'll have to pick a night that's on the dark of the moon," the other man said. "I'd sure hate for the cap'n to catch us takin' his rice."

"What you think he'd do to us?"

"Hang us on the nearest tree."

"Listen, Josh. They don't know that Father opposes hanging."

"He might *not* oppose hanging them if they stole the rice!"

The boys stood in silence, both thinking that they had to do something to stop the gangsters from stealing their father's rice.

Finally, Matt whispered, "Let's go, Josh. We know what they're planning, and we can work out some strategy to prevent them from being successful."

"And what might that be?"

"I don't know now, but it'll come to us I'm sure."

"I guess we'd better get away from here, but give me a moment to see if I can find the lizard."

"He could be a hundred miles from Hell Hole Swamp," Matt said.

"You're so encouraging!" Josh murmured, dropping his head. "I sure hope that snakebite didn't prevent me from ever seeing the lizard again."

"Something else would come along to attract your interest and you'd soon forget about it."

"Are you daft?" Josh asked, too loudly. "I'll never forget the lizard, and if you don't help me find him I'll never tell you where the sphinx is."

"Listen," one of the gangsters said. "I hear talkin'."

"Run, Matt!" Josh screamed. "Run for your life!"

The twins, swinging by their arms, hurried over the inlet and down the road, and they didn't slow down until they came to the haunted oak tree. Almost out of breath, they looked back and didn't see the men, but they didn't tarry and ran home as fast as their legs would carry them. As they approached the veranda, something was dreadfully wrong. A courier, who seemed weary, had slid off a horse that looked to be nearly dead, and when the messenger handed Mr. Bondurant a note, he read it and looked as though he became weak in the knees.

"What is it, Father?" Matt asked, as he ran to the porch. He took several deep breaths.

Mr. Bondurant looked at his son and the note slipped from his fingers. He picked it up and reread it. "Uncle Tidyman is dead, and Narcissa needs us in Charleston. It seems my sister not only has lost her husband, but he had just signed a promissory note, and she is about to lose her home."

"In other words, Uncle Tidyman borrowed money on his home, signed a note, and now he's dead and unable to pay the debt."

"Quite right, Matthew," Mr. Bondurant said.

Josh thought about the time that would be lost in

searching for the lizard if they had to go to Charleston, and Matt was thinking that it seemed the time would never come when he could continue his search for the sphinx, but at the time of a death in the family, southern people stuck together. They went inside to prepare for the journey to Charleston, not knowing how long they would be away, and hoping they would be at home when the rice was harvested and the family portion was stashed in the barn.

15

After the funeral at St. Michael's Church on Meeting Street, the family gathered in the morning room of the Tidyman home to talk about Narcissa's financial situation. Josh and Matt, in dark suits with vests, sat quietly as they took in the formality of the situation. Their mother sat on the other side of the room, quietly gazing from a window.

"I'll sign a promissory note to cover the indebtedness of Tidyman," Mr. Bondurant said to his sister.

Narcissa rushed across the carpet and kissed her brother on the cheek, then tipped back her head and clasped her hands in a gesture of gratitude. "You have taken my burden as your own. To become a widow is enough to bear without being threatened with losing one's home."

"Father, can we take Aunt Narcissa home with us?" Josh broke in quickly, thinking that they would leave for the plantation at an earlier time if they didn't have to remain in Charleston until she had resigned herself to her grief.

"Good idea, Josh," Matt said, feeling the very same sentiments as his twin.

Mrs. Bondurant rose and walked over to her sister-in-law. "I think the children have made a wonderful suggestion, Narcissa. We'd love for you to come home with us for a visit."

"Let's leave now," Josh chimed in.

Mr. Bondurant waved a hand in the air. "Have patience. Narcissa and I shall go to the lawyer's office on Broad Street tomorrow, and the day after that we'll go back to The Bond."

"Plan on spending several weeks with us," Mrs. Bondurant said as she went back to her chair. "It will do you good."

"I agree," Mr. Bondurant added. "The children are involved in a search for the sphinx, and maybe they will find it."

Narcissa fanned her face with a lace handkerchief, and said, "I remember Father saying there was a sphinx on the plantation, but he was never able to locate it."

"None of our ancestors ever found it," Mr. Bondurant agreed, "but this younger generation may prove to be more clever than any of them. It would not surprise me if Joshua and Matthew come up with a clue."

Matt shot his eyes toward Josh, but the expression on Josh's face told his twin to keep quiet about the clue. This was *not* the time.

Later, as Josh and Matt meandered along Tradd Street toward the harbor, Josh said, "I'm glad Aunt Narcissa's going to visit us at The Bond. She'll keep Father so busy talking he won't have time to check on you and me." He slapped his brother on the shoulder, knowingly.

But Matt didn't feel at all playful about getting on with the project. "If you would give up on Hell Hole Swamp and concentrate on finding the sphinx, Father's attention would not bother you." Matt's patience was wearing thin, waiting for Josh to tell him the clue to the whereabouts of the sphinx. "It's maddening. I don't know how much more time I can spend going to that ghastly swamp when we could be finding the sphinx."

But Josh didn't allow his brother's complaints to faze him. "And I cannot wait to go back to Hell Hole Swamp."

He didn't have long to wait. In three days he was again hurrying along The Shadows on the way to the dark and foreboding place.

"If we don't see the lizard today, I am giving up," Matt argued. "This venture is useless and we're squandering valuable time. You know we don't have too long before we have to leave for England."

"Don't fret. We shall see the lizard today." To try to get his brother's mind off the topic of abandoning the search for the lizard and raccoon, Josh changed the subject. "Do you really want to go to Cambridge?"

"It will prepare us for everything we want from life," Matt said, "but there's a part of me wishing we could put off going this year."

Josh hadn't thought of postponing the trip to England. "Would Father let us wait another year?"

"As sure as the moon shines on the Cooper River he'll make us go *this* year. That's his major interest right now. Yours is the lizard, mine is the sphinx, and his is our education in England."

Josh thought that Matt was right. Their father would never let them wait another year. "Race you to the swamp."

But before Josh broke into a run, Matt cautioned, "Better not make any noise. If the gangsters are there we'll have to get gone before they notice us."

"Those gangsters aren't going to prevent me from seeing the lizard if he's there," Josh said. "I may have to tread lightly, but I'm taking the time for a quick look."

The twins were almost on tiptoe as they came to the swamp.

"You see anybody?" Josh asked.

"No," Matt whispered. "But don't make any noise. They could be lying in wait for us."

"As the old saying goes, 'Don't worry worry 'til worry worries you,'" Josh said. "I'm going across the water."

Matt's eyes searched the dark and gloomy landscape but he saw nothing out of the ordinary. "Suppose I'll have to come too, but be ready for a fast getaway if we see anyone."

Within seconds Josh had crossed the water, dropped down on the mudbank, and was looking around. Seeing nothing unusual, he felt perfectly safe. "I'm crossing the next lagoon."

"Don't be too hasty. The men could be lurking somewhere, watching us."

"You don't have to go, but *I'm* going." When Josh was on the far side of the second arm of water, he called back. "I don't see a thing, and I don't hear anything. Come on over."

After a moment Matt had also crossed over, and when he dropped to the ground and looked around, he said, "It's obvious the lizard and raccoon are gone. Let's get away from here."

Josh thought over the words he'd just heard. It *was* likely such a lizard would not select a place like Hell Hole Swamp for a permanent home but would live in sort of den, at a place that was isolated and secure, a place not visited by gangsters or anyone else. But never to see the lizard again would be so disappointing. He flopped down on the mudbank. "I just hate to give up. We cannot ever tell a living soul what we saw at Hell Hole Swamp."

"We saw something, and now we have to forget it," Matt declared. "Put it out of our minds." He snapped his fingers in the air. "Just like that."

"It's the end of the universe," Josh said, feeling that it was the very end of the most exciting experience of his life. He had become attached to the lizard, as dangerous as such a huge animal could be. Nothing in his life had ever been so invigorating as slipping away to Hell Hole Swamp and finding the largest lizard known to mankind. "I don't know what the worst part of it will be," he finally said. "Trying to put what I've seen out of my mind, or retaining it in my memory and not saying a word about it."

"You might not live to say anything about what you've seen here," a man snarled as he stepped from behind a tree.

Josh's eyes quickly took in the situation, and he saw no quick means of escape.

A second man joined his friend just as Matt screamed, "It's the gangsters!"

"We were not talking about you," Josh said, his voice low and hoarse and his eyelids not fully open.

The first gangster moved in front of Josh and faced him squarely. Without taking his eyes off Josh's steady gaze, he slowly squatted down so that he could pull a knife from his high-topped shoe. Josh thought that he had never in his life been so afraid. He could feel his heart beating in his throat, and his mouth was suddenly dry and his tongue stuck to the roof of his mouth. *He couldn't talk.*

Attempting to use the intelligence that his family gave him credit for, Matt was furiously trying to think of some way to outsmart the men, but he concluded there was no way out of this situation. They couldn't run, for they were surrounded by trees and water, and the twins were no match for the hoodlums when it came to fighting. As Matt thought about it, he couldn't remember hearing about a Bondurant being engaged in a fight as they depended on their intellect to get themselves out of unpleasant predicaments.

"What are we going to do, Matt?" Josh squeaked right out loud, his voice still not working right. He didn't care if the men knew he was frightened nearly to death of them. The man staring at him was waving the knife in front of his face, and the shiny blade glistened in a shaft of sunlight. Josh thought that the knife was the only thing about the men that was clean, and then he wondered why such a thought entered his head at this very moment. Be it clean or dirty, that knife could slit his throat in a flash. Instinctively, he moved back.

"You're the sons of the cap'n," the man with the knife said.

The twins didn't answer, and the other man growled, "They're the ones, all right."

"You heard us talking when you were here before," the man with the knife spat. "You know we plan to use the barn key, and you know what we are going to do. If we let you get away, you'll tell the cap'n, if you haven't told him already."

"We haven't told Father anything," Josh said. "Honest. We haven't told anybody that we ever saw you."

"Oh no?" the second gangster asked sarcastically. "I don't believe a word of that."

"It's true," Matt insisted. "We are not supposed to come here, for the very reason that we might encounter the likes of you. We would be punished if our parents knew we came here."

The second gangster squared off in front of Matt. "Then the only thing to do is make sure that you don't decide to talk too much at some later time. Your mouth has to be permanently closed."

"Oh, no," Josh called out. "Please don't kill us."

"What would you gain by killing us?" Matt asked.

"For one thing, the cap'n won't know who stole his rice," the man with the knife said through his teeth.

Josh was thinking that his father already knew the killers came here, but it would do no good to try to reason with the men. He and Matt were as good as dead now, and there was nothing they could do about it.

"You grab that one and I'll take this one," the second man said as he took hold of Matt's arm. Matt jerked away and jumped for a tree limb, but the man pulled him back, wrestled him to the wet ground, and held him there.

Josh yelled as loudly as he could. *"Help!"* But even as he screamed, he knew there was no one to hear him. They were too far from any part of the plantation where people worked. The man with the knife was standing immediately in front of him and held the knife up to Josh's face.

"Please don't kill my brother," Matt cried. "He hasn't done anything."

A wave of emotion flooded Josh's whole body as he heard Matt pleading for his life, and he wished he'd listened to Matt and gone in search of the sphinx.

Still holding the knife by Josh's face, the criminal backed him into the edge of the water, taking slow, deliberate steps. Josh knew the end of his life was near, but he thought that perhaps Matt could escape. "Matt, I'm going to make both of them fight me and you make a run for it."

The man put the knife between his teeth and held Josh's arms with a steel grip. "You think it'll take two to do the job? Boy, you're senseless. Either one of us could kill you with a hand tied behind his back."

Suddenly, something from above came down in the narrow space between Josh and the gangster and the man fell back. "Wha'?"

Josh looked around in surprise but saw nothing.

The man, writhing in pain, was able to pull himself to the mudbank.

The other man turned loose of Matt. "Wha' happened?"

"Something hit my arms so hard it cut them. I believe my arms are broken."

The other man ran to the injured gangster and leaned over him, looking at the bloody arms. Just at that moment, the thing that had come down from above emerged from the murky water, went high in the air, and crashed down on the neck of the man leaning over his friend. He fell on top of the man covered in blood and his neck appeared to be broken.

"What is it, Matt?" Josh called out. "What's happening?"

"I don't know. Do you see anything?"

Josh turned, and not far away stood the lizard, his tail curved and whipping the men who were already more than half-dead. "Look! Matt, it's the lizard!"

Matt's eyes became soulful and his expression sensitive. "The lizard saved our lives."

Josh's face was set in questioning lines, and a muscle twitched in his temple. He squeezed his eyes tightly shut. The lizard had actually come to their rescue and *had,* as Matt said, saved their lives. He had known for the longest time that the lizard was a friend, but it had seemed too incredible to be true. The animal was a creature of the wild and knew nothing of the world of the twins, and yet it had established some sort of bond from which a kind of friendship sprang, and then it had saved their lives.

By now the men were completely helpless, and Josh motioned for Matt to join him as he walked toward the lizard, which was standing on its back feet and scrutinizing the twins.

"Remember, Josh," Matt warned, "the lizard is a wild animal, and dangerous. Be careful."

Josh observed Matt out of the corner of an eye. "Horsefeathers! He's the best friend we ever had. He gave us back our lives when the intruders were ready to kill us."

"He's pleasant enough, and he *did* save our lives, but he could be sucking us in. Don't let him win you over, Josh, until you're sure it's safe."

Josh flushed and retorted, "What an ungrateful goose you are! What does somebody have to do to win *you* over? Are you skeptical of *everyone*?"

"I just don't want to hear your hollering when the lizard grabs you," Matt answered, then concentrated on his brother with renewed interest. "I'll admit this—the lizard feels close to you. That's evident."

At that moment, the lizard made a faint grunting sound, and extended itself toward Josh.

"He's coming to you," Matt cautioned, but just at that moment the lizard turned to a root where the raccoon was making its way toward the lizard's hand.

The lizard lifted the raccoon and offered it to Josh.

"He's giving the raccoon to me," Josh said, his eyes wide. "I want to take it, but I shouldn't try to take it away from the lizard. Each one would miss the other."

"The raccoon is close to the lizard," Matt stated. "No question about that. But I think the lizard wants you to hold the raccoon. Wait," Matt said, not taking his eyes off the lizard's face. "I think the reptile is trying to tell you something."

Although the lizard's arms were short, he extended a three-fingered hand toward the raccoon and then toward Josh.

"Josh, the lizard wants you to keep the raccoon. Go on and take the animal."

Josh looked at the lizard, and the strange smile was playing on its face.

"Take the raccoon," Matt urged.

Josh looked at the raccoon. It had grown since he had seen it. He took it and nudged the back of its neck.

"Josh."

"What?"

"Look at the lizard. I believe he has just told you farewell, and the raccoon is a kind of consolation gift."

The lizard was slowly backing away, and within minutes its form had blended perfectly with the surroundings and the twins could not see it.

Although Josh and Matt didn't look at each other, surprise was in their eyes. Josh finally spoke, interrupting his brother's contemplations. "As he was leaving, he had the most conciliatory expression. He was reluctant to go, but the time had come."

"What do you make of it, Josh?"

"This isn't the lizard's home, and both of us have known that. He was only passing through, and after he discovered us and the raccoon, he decided to stay a while."

"He saw us and made friends, as much as a lizard can," Matt added, picking up the story.

"He kept us safe while he was at the swamp, but now he's gone away and we are likely never to see him again," Josh commented.

"True. But I'll never forget him, especially that tail. That tail saved our lives. Did you look at it? I mean *really* look at it, Josh?"

Josh scratched the raccoon's neck and it nuzzled up to him. "It looked like a black rope that got smaller and smaller until at the end it was no bigger than a string. But all the way down a brilliant green stripe was on the top."

"That glossy, green stripe extended to the very end," Matt concurred.

Just then the boys' eyes fell on the gangsters, who appeared to be dead, and they knew there was a question that had to be resolved.

"What do you think we should do?" Josh asked.

"Leave them behind," Matt said. "We're going home

now, and we'll never come back here. As the time passes, we'll look back on Hell Hole Swamp, the lizard, and the gangsters and view it as we see a dream. We'll think we know what really happened, but we won't be sure. We shall probably come to doubt that any of it happened at all."

Walking home, the twins knew that one of the most dramatic parts of their lives had come to a close. They had discovered a lizard that was larger than anyone's imagination, and not only had it become their friend, it had saved their lives.

A deer pranced into the roadway, and the way it looked at Josh and Matt left no doubt that it considered them intruders.

"Wild animals can be friendly only to a degree," Matt observed. "But they will always be true to their nature. Always wild."

"Just the same," Josh answered, "I wish from the depths of my heart that I could return the favor, do something for the lizard who saved our lives."

"It's not likely that opportunity will be afforded us," Matt responded.

"Joshua. Matthew. Where did you get that raccoon?" Mr. Bondurant asked his sons when they walked up the steps to their home.

"We found it in a ditch," Josh answered.

"Well, build a pen," his father directed. "And when it's a little older, turn it back toward the woods."

There was no suspicion in Mr. Bondurant's voice, and Josh and Matt felt no need to give any further details or make an explanation.

16

IT WAS EASY TO SEE that Josh and Matt were Bondurants as they strolled toward the towers near the rice fields in search of the sphinx. They bore the strong, determined look of their father and his father before him, a man who they had been told had been much like the earliest Bondurant to come to South Carolina, William the First. It was he who had given the plantation the name The Bond, and he also had proclaimed that the name signified not only the family seat but a sort of covenant that embraced all of the future members of that distinguished family. Any Bondurant who inherited the plantation would also inherit the responsibility for seeing that the place was kept in perfect order and the family name remained free of any blemishes. The covenant, although it had not been chiseled in stone, had endured.

Suddenly Matt's eyes were like darting snakes and his words sidled over to Josh. "Tell me the clues to the location of the sphinx."

"Don't be in such haste. I'll tell you when we arrive at the scene."

"Stop right there!" Matt felt like kicking himself for waiting so long to be told the clue. "If you think I'm going to take one more step before you tell me, you are mistaken."

"Are you the impatient one!" Josh scowled. "But what's

the difference if I tell you now or later?" A rush of warmth suddenly flowed through his body as he thought about sharing the clue of the sphinx with his twin.

"I should have challenged you before now and made you confess to all you know," Matt said.

"We had the lizard to be concerned about," Josh reminded his brother. "Now is the time for the sphinx."

"Where is it?" Matt asked, his mind working swiftly.

Josh jerked a thumb in the direction of the river. "We don't have to stop here in the road to talk. Keep moving."

"Get on with it!"

Josh thought back to the beginning of his research, and he wanted to tell Matt everything he could remember. His manner was more genial than ever as he began. "From all I could learn of the sphinxes in Greece and other places, they are large, so we can assume that this one is a huge statue."

Matt already knew this. "Go on."

"And there are few places on a plantation such as ours where a huge statue could be concealed."

"I know," Matt agreed. "But *where* could it be?"

Josh waved a hand. "Don't be impatient. Let me explain all of it."

"I'm waiting," Matt's voice all but rang out.

"Not only is the statue huge, it is in a crouching position."

"How do you know?"

"Because that is the way sphinxes are. The head of the creature, be it man or woman, is the highest point, and the creature is resting on its legs, with the front feet outstretched."

"If it is in a crouching position, then it can't be very tall," Matt surmised.

"It is as big as our house!" Josh was about to lose patience with his skeptical brother.

"The mansion?"

"Absolutely."

"How harebrained do you think I am?" Matt responded, looking in the distance, his shoulders hunched in concentration.

"You are not harebrained at all," Josh answered, clearing his throat. "You just haven't spent as many hours thinking about this as I have."

Matt stiffened. Josh was intent on stringing out this explanation, and he was being downright obnoxious. But Matt decided not to allow Josh to get his goat, and he said in an even voice, "All right. Go on."

"There is another thing. All sphinxes face a river. At least the ones I read about faced rivers or deltas."

Matt's eyes narrowed as they sized up his brother. "That's the only clue you have given me. Now I know that the sphinx faces the Cooper River. But I have no idea where something as big as a house could possibly be concealed. And if you want to know the truth, I don't believe *you* know where it is."

A smile played on Josh's lips. "I know where it is all right, and it is so obvious I cannot for the life of me figure out why our ancestors could not locate it."

Just then the twins passed the cemetery that had been cleaned, and they quickly glanced around. Although the work on the burial ground had been completed, someone had left a hoe lying on the ground. "You think we should take that hoe with us?" Josh asked.

"If we need it one of us can come back for it," Matt replied.

Within minutes the twins stood at the foot of the high hill on which the towers stood.

"Matt?"

"Yes?"

"You are looking at the only place on the plantation where a sphinx could be located."

"There?"

"Right in front of you, under the towers, covered in dirt."

"Precisely," Matt answered, emphasizing each syllable.

"The sphinx is under the towers," Josh said, driving home the conclusion.

"And when our great-great-grandfather wanted to construct the towers on the highest possible elevation on the plantation, he realized the sphinx was the only thing of such height."

"And so he covered it with mud, clay, sand, anything he could get his hands on, until it was completely covered, and then he had the towers constructed on the firmest of foundations," Josh explained.

"And the sphinx made a perfect foundation for such heavy towers," Matt added.

"There is something else," Josh said, with cool authority. "As the face is toward the river, that means two huge paws are also in that direction."

Matt's eyes danced. "Now if we can figure out how to get rid of some of the hard-packed earth we can expose enough of the sphinx to show Father."

"I'll go back to the cemetery and get the hoe," Josh offered.

Matt started toward the hill. "I'm going to find those paws."

"Remember, Twin," Josh said as a parting shot. "A sphinx is a place of burial, and the inside of the statue is a tomb."

Matt turned to face Josh. "That means maybe somewhere on a side of the hill there is a door, or entrance to the statue. Unless our great-great-grandfather covered it while building the mound."

Josh slapped his knee and laughed uproariously. "That's right. I hadn't thought of a door. We could even go inside."

Matt lowered his brows. "Are you sure you want to? There would be a bone or two in there."

"Even if we were afraid to go inside, we could at least look for the door and have a peek."

"Go and get the hoe," Matt cut off Josh's thoughts. "I'll figure out where to start our dig."

"What if we find some jewels in there?" Josh asked over a shoulder as he ran toward the cemetery. "Jewels were buried with the corpses in Greece."

"You'd better hope you don't come face-to-face with a skeleton or a ghost in there!" Matt yelled.

While Josh was gone, Matt concentrated on where to start digging. Picturing the head of the sphinx high in the air, he concluded the paws would be about twelve feet below the top of the mound, and by the time Josh had returned with the hoe, Matt was standing on the side of the hill facing the river. "Bring me the hoe. I'm going to start here."

"This is very hush-hush," Josh said breathlessly as he hurried toward his brother. "We don't want to say anything about the sphinx until we are sure we have found it."

"If you have steered me in the right direction, it won't be long before we can tell," Matt declared. "Our lips are forever sealed against revealing the giant lizard, but I intend to blurt out everything I know about the sphinx." His stare into the distance intensified and he frowned and shook his head. "I can see Father now when we tell him. It will be one of the most extraordinary days of his life."

Matt and Josh worked at a high pitch, and late in the day they were about to give up hope of finding anything when the hoe struck a hard object.

"Move back!" Josh ordered his brother. Josh fell down on his knees and frantically dug away dirt with his bare hands, breaking fingernails and cutting his fingers but not aware of the pain. He believed with all his heart they had found the sphinx.

17

"DO YOU *REALLY* BELIEVE we have found the sphinx?" Josh asked as he and Matt flew toward the towers the next morning. Not awaiting a reply, he added, "You certainly knew how to persuade Father to let us come back here today. For a minute I thought he would insist we stay home."

"The sphinx is the only subject we are interested in and Father knows it," Matt reasoned. "And as our time on the plantation is so limited, he didn't want to deprive us of our search, especially after I told him we believed we had a clue."

"In truth, Father doesn't believe we have a ghost of a chance of locating the sphinx," Josh said.

"True. And that is one reason I shall be so pleased to announce the discovery to him."

"Father wants us to enjoy our family life until we leave and he would be guilt-ridden if he did anything to deprive us during our last days on the plantation," Josh chattered, mostly to himself.

Matt answered, "We must never let Father notice how sad it makes us to leave the plantation."

"He probably knows it," Josh concluded, "but it would kill him if he we didn't go to Cambridge."

"Father would never be the Bondurant who broke the rules of the old covenant, and I think it states that sons of Bondurants be educated in England."

"Covenant? Is that the yellowed, brittle paper Father keeps in the walnut secretary?" Josh asked.

"It's one and the same, although it's not very official. All it is is some notes scribbled down by the first Bondurant, the one who carved the plantation out of the wilderness."

"Goodness me," Josh said. "I had forgotten about that old document." After a moment he had another thought. "Do you think he, the first Bondurant, could be the one who had the sphinx built?"

"Who knows?" Matt answered as his mind returned to the present. "Race you to the towers."

The twins didn't stop running until they stood under the brick cylinders looming above them, like columns on a Greek mountain.

Josh grabbed the hoe and started toward their dig, with Matt trailing in his wake.

Handing the hoe to Matt, Josh again dug away dirt with his bare hands, and the paw was becoming more visible. Matt's mind, so agile and astute, leaped ahead. He knew without having to dig where the other paw was, and he could picture the two sphinx feet, in a perfect line, pointing toward the river.

"Josh! How about if I dig at the site of the other paw?"

Before Josh had time to answer, he cut a finger. Ignoring the pain, he examined the object and saw the end of an oyster shell protruding from the concrete. "Look! It's an oyster shell."

"Indeed. We knew the sphinx was made of tabby," Matt responded.

Their curiosity aroused, Matt abandoned the idea of digging for the other paw, and he joined his brother, who was removing dirt more furiously than ever. Finally Josh stopped digging and fell back on the ground for a rest. He let his eyes gaze at the blue sky with a few soft clouds near the horizon. The sky looked so peaceful, so gentle in the morning light. There was such comfort and tranquility here. How homesick he would be for this place after he left. So many things had fired his imagination from earliest childhood, but nothing had ever flamed it as much as the giant lizard and the sphinx. He would never relish anything in England as he had the adventures of the past weeks. He rose up on an elbow and thought that he and Matt would be fortunate if they made all the discoveries about the sphinx before they sailed down to Charleston and off toward England. Just then he noticed Matt, who hadn't let up in his digging with the hoe. It was surprising to see Matt exert himself to such an extent. He was much like one of the plantation workhorses.

Anxiety was rising in Matt. There were no two ways about it. They had found the sphinx, but he wondered how long it would take them to dig away enough dirt to reveal a portion of it as proof. Leaning forward on the handle of the hoe, he took a deep breath. "Do you think we should ask for help?"

Josh looked at his brother uncomprehendingly, his dark brows drawn together in a frown. He was thunderstruck that his twin would consider such a thing. "Ridiculous!"

"But we could dig for days on end and not come up with a whole paw. On the other hand, if some of the people from the fields and carpenter shop helped us, we could uncover a goodly portion of the statue much sooner."

"Why are you in such a rush, for heaven's sake?" Josh asked.

"Why *not,* for heaven's sake?"

Josh's lips drew together in aggravation as a thought struck him. "I truly hope you haven't mentioned the sphinx to anyone. Could this sudden and rather stupid decision of yours mean that you have already asked for assistance?"

"Don't get so het up. Of course I haven't said anything about the sphinx to anyone."

Josh stood up and flexed his muscles. "We have to be sensible about this and not make rash decisions. There will be enough time for arguments after we decide to tell Father about the sphinx. When and where is something we have to settle. We must work even harder so that time will arrive more quickly."

Matt gave the ground a chop with the hoe. "Bondurant blood flows through your veins, that's for sure." He took several deep breaths and brought a neutral expression to his face. "We are so close, and yet exposing the statue seems so far beyond our reach."

Josh's mind went back to the past. "Think of all the people before us who have searched for the sphinx and were not successful. At least we are going in the right direction." Then, as he studied a part of the object that had just been revealed by Matt's digging, he squealed, "Look! It's a curve that was formed by human hands."

"You are right," Matt said, "but I am going to die of heart failure if I have to work this hard much longer."

"And I am going to die of heart failure if we don't soon expose a large portion of the paw," Josh shot back.

The twins were shaken, and their senses were swimming.

Digging again with his hands, Josh asked, "Do you believe there is such a thing as a second wind?"

"I truly hope so," Matt answered, breathlessly. "I am ready for it now."

"Look," Josh said suddenly. "It's a toe!"

"It *is*," Matt agreed.

Josh laughed with such merriment tears sprang to his eyes. Recovering, he flicked the tears away with his dirt-covered fingertips.

"All of our suspicions are confirmed," Matt said, and he let out a yell that was not characteristic of him. After a moment, he fell back on the ground and closed his eyes, thinking, analyzing. There had been nagging questions hanging in the air, but he let go of them. This *was* the sphinx. Josh had been amazingly correct in his collection and analysis of clues. The sphinx did indeed face the Cooper River and delta, and they had uncovered a portion of one of the paws.

Even though Josh and Matt had often opposed each other, there was a special bond between them, the bond that exists between twins, and it had never been more binding than at that moment.

"What should we do?" Josh asked.

"Let us walk around, relax a little, and do nothing rash," Matt suggested. "To be rash and obsessive is silly."

Josh led the way. "From my research on sphinxes, I learned that some people are completely captivated, ensnared even, by them. There is enormous pull there, and passion. We must be careful not to become prisoners of the spell."

"Very clever of you, brother," Matt called out. "But to tell you the truth, I believe both of us are under the spell already. For the rest of our lives we shall look back on this moment and remember clearly every detail. That is why I think it is important that we do nothing foolish and weaken the impact of the discovery."

"When do you think we should make the announcement?" Josh asked.

"Let us say nothing to anyone today, and tomorrow, as we chip away and expose an even larger portion of the paw, we will decide exactly how to tell Father."

"Let's go home and sleep on it," Josh answered.

18

After a restless night of tossing and turning, the twins had risen earlier than usual, but they had been extraordinarily careful not to let anyone notice their excitement. As they made their way down the sandy lane, they were relieved to be away from the mansion and yet concerned about the people within it.

"We have to talk with Father about the sphinx, or we will have serious problems later, trying to explain all of it," Matt said, as he kicked a pinecone out of the lane.

Josh nodded agreement. "We should let Father in on it after today's dig. He will scarcely be able to take it in."

They walked until the river was within sight, and it was a heavenly day, the beginning of the most absorbing experience of their lives, the twins were thinking. The sky was full of sunshine and the Cooper River was brilliant. Full-grown oak trees were brightly green, the branches heavily laden with undulating gray moss. Although Matt and Josh had not had the most restful of nights, they were alert, refreshed, and anxious to get started on the dig.

"Today is a time to look into our future," Matt finally remarked. "What happens today will be something to tell our children and grandchildren. As people who share in this property, they will also share in the sphinx."

Josh didn't respond for a while, and then he said,

"Although we think of the sphinx as ours, it will belong to everybody. It is such a historic statue that people from everywhere will come to see it, and of course it will be in the ownership of those who own The Bond."

Matt nodded, and the twins exchanged long, very knowing gazes, remembering one of the strictest rules of The Bond. Mr. Bondurant had told them they must always care for the plantation in every way and share it with others, never closing ranks to protect the family.

"Father always emphasizes the Scripture that says much is expected of those who receive much. To live at The Bond is to receive much," Matt went on, "and now we have an opportunity to give something of inestimable value to the whole country—the sphinx."

"Come on," Josh said, sprinting ahead. "Talking about the sphinx is not getting us anywhere." When they reached the site, he took the hoe from a pine tree against which it was propped, and handed it to Matt, who approached the dig with large, leaping steps.

An hour later Josh was exhausted. He straightened and gazed at the paw.

Matt stopped hoeing, turned, and looked at his brother, expectancy and warmth filling his face. "How are we doing, Birdbrain?"

"Believe it or not, it is shaping up to be a sphinx. We have been *working*!"

Matt blinked his eyes rapid-fire several times. "I think it is time to look at something else for a change. Even when I close my eyes I see the paw."

"Bright idea," Josh agreed. "Want to run around the path at the bottom of the hill and give our legs a workout?"

"*Run!*" Matt sprinted off.

When Matt struck out around the pathway that had emerged at the foot of the small mountain during their exploration, Josh yelled, "Brain, steady on. You're going to soar right up and over the towers if you don't slow down."

"Oh, come on. You talk like you are weak."

"Scraping away dirt is just as tiring as hoeing. Slow down."

The twins slackened their pace and looked around. Although the sun had come out from behind a bank of leaden clouds making its way across the river, the day had turned blustery, and leaves and pine needles swirled around the boys' feet.

"What do you think will happen after we announce our discovery?" Josh asked, kicking leaves away from his feet.

"As sure as my name is Matthew Bondurant, the Alstons will arrive from Waccamaw, the Rhetts from Charleston, and the Izards from Goose Creek. The sphinx will be a state attraction."

"You think so?" Josh queried, his eyes on the side of the hill, about midway between the front and back.

"I *know* so. Not only those families, but the Fripps will travel from Beaufort, and the Joneses from Savannah, and everybody will want to see the statue modeled after the one in Egypt."

Josh didn't answer.

"The Bond has always been noted for its beauty and size, and now we have a priceless sculpture to share. Our fortune is bountiful, wouldn't you say?"

Josh still didn't answer, and Matt looked at him. "Are you not paying attention to what I am saying?"

Still, Josh said nothing.

"You are preoccupied, and for what reason, for heaven's sake?"

Finally, Josh said, "Either my mind has gone numb, or there is an opening in the side of the hill."

"There does seem to be something there," Matt agreed. "But it is nearly concealed by weeds, bushes, and other growth." He walked closer.

"Matt, be careful. If there is an opening to the inside of the tomb, there is no telling what is inside."

"Stay in your tracks and do not take your eyes off the opening," Matt said. "I am going back for the hoe and poke around inside."

"Do you think that is safe?"

"Safe or not, it is something I have to do," Matt replied as he left.

While his brother was gone, Josh didn't remove his vision from the opening in the side of the hill. Suddenly he turned pale and went weak in the knees. More than anything, he desired to sit on the ground but forced himself to stand. Never in his life had he been so weak.

When Matt returned, Josh took him aside. "There is something you must know, and I pray to God I have the strength to tell you."

"Josh! What has happened to you? You look like a ghost!"

"I feel like a ghost. In fact, I may *be* a ghost at this very moment. I am certainly not a part of this world."

Matt threw down the hoe. "I've got to get you home."

"No. I must tell you something, and it is surely the most difficult thing I have ever had to do. If I owned The Bond, I'd give it away if it would substitute for my having to tell you this."

"Josh, what is it?"

"Matt," Josh began, "to find something as rare and historical as the sphinx is memorable, but only to us. We have lost our lifetime of celebration over the discovery, for we can never disclose the location of the sphinx to a living and breathing soul." Josh took a step back, waiting for his brother's reaction, aware that he would be angrier than ever, but he had to be told.

"You are mad!"

"I am not mad, Matt, and I can prove it. Come with me."

Matt followed as Josh took him toward the very doorlike aperture in the side of the hill.

"I don't know what you are saying," Matt spat, "but if you think for one minute that I am not going to tell Father of this discovery you are going to spend the rest of your days at the house for the insane."

Now at the door, Josh pointed to the ground. As clear as anything, from the opening and extending for a few

feet outside, was what appeared to be a black rope that got smaller and smaller until it was no larger than a string at the end, and a stripe of brightest green was on the top.

"The tomb of the sphinx is the home of the lizard," Matt whispered, incredulously.

Josh tugged his dazed brother well away from the hole.

"And we can never tell a living soul. The lizard saved our lives, and to tell where his den is would be to take away his life."

"What a bloody deal! *Our sphinx!* I have never heard of anything so outrageous in my life. Can you imagine, as hard as we worked!" Matt's mouth worked with sudden disgust as he thought of the futility of their labors. "When Father showed us the old map, and told us it was conceivable that the sphinx was here, we believed through hard work, effort, brilliance, all of that, we could find it. 'Oh, really,' Father was probably thinking. 'You young fellows think *you* can find it when others could not?' And we found it, and now we cannot tell it. It is just so ridiculous, and out of the question. It is just such a cruel end to our efforts."

"Like you, I think the others thought we could not do it," Josh remarked. "And we did. And now we cannot tell them." He paused. "But it is something wonderful for us to keep between us. Twins have secrets that they do not share with others, and do we have a secret!"

"If there was any way, any way under the sun that we could tell it, I would. I'd tell it as soon as I could get home."

"Matt! Don't even entertain such a thought. Think what the lizard did for us."

"That lizard. I didn't want to look for it in the first place. If we had never gone back to Hell Hole Swamp, and had come here in search of the sphinx, we could tell everything." Matt eyed his brother curiously. "And I just might do that anyway."

"Oh no you don't!" Josh leaned toward his brother and his stare intensified. "Not unless you want me to commit murder. Even the most genteel people can commit murder. And I could be capable of it under such circumstances." Josh paused and bit his lip. "And remember this. You brought me the books on Egypt and asked me to look for clues to the location of the sphinx, and I did search for clues, and I am the one who knew where the statue was, not you." Josh was surprised at how tight his throat was, and how his stomach lurched at the very thought of his twin brother disclosing the whereabouts of the sphinx. "I sincerely hope you give this serious thought and come to the right conclusion."

"If we cannot tell anyone about the discovery of the sphinx, then we cannot ever come here again," Matt answered.

"Why?" Josh asked.

"The lizard was our friend for a short time, when it was away from its den, but in its established home within the sphinx, we would not be welcome. From now on, the lizard is off-limits to us."

Josh made no response. He looked at Matt full in the face and it seemed as though an immense change had occurred in the passing of only a few seconds, a change that would endure for the rest of their lives. They were Bondurants, and they were true to their heritage. To be honest and fair was a part of their innermost being, and when it came down to it, Matt could not have revealed the information about the sphinx any more than Josh could, Josh believed.

Matt picked up the hoe and threw it into the bushes. "Let's go home. Our next adventure will be in England, and that will be no more enduring than finding the sphinx."

"I wish we didn't have to go to England," Josh agreed, "but I have no intention of telling that to Father."

When Josh and Matt returned home, Mr. Bondurant was standing at the entrance to the drawing room, a formal reception room that he used for family consultations only during the most serious of times. He asked his sons to come inside.

Matt and Josh eyed each other. *Did their father know of*

their discovery? Had he heard that they had visited Hell Hole Swamp?

The twins sat on a damask sofa, under portraits of Bondurants long buried in the family plot at Goose Creek Church. Mrs. Bondurant and Narcissa sat on chairs near a window.

Mr. Bondurant threw his sons an apologetic smile as he strode to the carved mantel. "It is such a pity that I have to tell you this," he said to his sons, giving them a fearful look through narrowed blue eyes. "As you know, I signed a promissory note for Narcissa, assuring that all of her debts would be paid. As it turns out, the debts are far more extensive than any of us had imagined, and it is going to take all of my assets for this year to satisfy the debts." He shifted on his feet, surveying the room, as his sons listened attentively. "As difficult as it is for me to tell you this, I shall come right to the point."

"Oh, no," Narcissa called out, putting a handkerchief to her eyes. "There must be another way."

"Be quiet, Narcissa. You know my decision. I am a man of honor."

"What is it, Father?" Matt queried.

"Your education at Cambridge will have to be postponed for one year."

"You mean we won't have to go to England this year?" Josh asked, a smile spreading across his lips.

"That is precisely what I mean, son. But things will be different next year, and we shall sail for England then."

"Father," Matt said, in mock seriousness, "please have no concern for Josh and me. Although we look forward to furthering our education there, we feel a mite immature this year, and next year would be the proper time for us to leave the plantation."

"Do you *truly* feel that way?" Mr. Bondurant asked.

"Of course we do, Father," Matt responded.

"What marvelous sons I have."

"I want to go to England next year," Josh chimed in. "There are some things we want to do here on the plantation. Although Matt and I have decided not to pursue the search for the sphinx, there are lots of other wonders at this place, yet to be discovered."

"That's right," Matt agreed. "The sphinx holds no attraction for us now, but we are already thinking of other things, such as..." He glanced at Josh for help in disclosing what other things they were interested in. As they had spent so much time discussing their departure for England, they had not thought of any plantation adventures yet to be discovered.

Did his sons have the intelligence to accept the inevitable so gracefully? Mr. Bondurant was wondering. They were true Bondurants! And of course they would behave like the great patrician gentlemen they would become.

"Father," Josh said, breaking into his thoughts, "what is that old story about jack-o'-lanterns?"

"Some people say they have seen them in the rice fields," Mr. Bondurant explained.

"What are they?" Matt asked.

"Who knows?" Mr. Bondurant answered. "They are said to be some weird presence that glows from the inside, neck to ankles."

"Have they been seen often?" Matt asked.

"Many times," his father said. "But no one knows what they are."

Matt's eyes connected with Josh's and there was a bond there, as strong as the name of their plantation and family. It is known only to twins.

EPILOGUE

AN ANCIENT RECORD indicates that a tabby sphinx exists somewhere on the coast of South Carolina. The location is unknown.

National Examiner, November 29, 1988

Indeed, since the end of June—when teenager Chris Davis spotted the first Lizard Man of the season near Scape Ore Swamp in Lee County, South Carolina—a staggering number of creature sightings have been reported across America.

Lizard Man, described by Davis and other witnesses as seven feet tall with green, scaly skin, red eyes, and three toes on each foot, is probably related to Bigfoot, Beckjord notes. [Erik Beckjord is the founder of the National Cryptozoological Society, an organization that investigates sightings of seemingly mythical monsters.]

The State, Columbia, South Carolina, July 19, 1988

Residents of the Browntown section of Lee County are abuzz about the "Lizard Man" ever since Tom and Mary Waye's car got "chewed up" sometime Thursday night, and Chris Davis got attacked several weeks ago.

"We've got a Bigfoot over here," Sheriff Liston Truesdale

said Monday with a chuckle. "It's the beatin'est thing I've ever seen."

Deputy Chester Lighty, who patrols Browntown, said he's heard talk of the "Lizard Man" for about three weeks. Two men told him a "creature" chased them from the swamp as they were getting water from a spring.

Davis said his car was attacked by the creature as he was replacing a flat tire along Browntown Road about 2 A.M. "It was green, wetlike, about 7 feet tall and had three fingers, red eyes, skin like a lizard, snakelike scales," Davis said Monday.

It caught up with him as he hit 40 mph, but only scratched the bumper.

Talk intensified Friday when the Wayes found their LTD with battered chrome, detached molding, wires pulled out of the engine and a broken hood ornament. "I hope nothing don't come back," Mrs. Waye said.

The State, Columbia, South Carolina,
July 20, 1988

Scape Ore Swamp was swamped Tuesday with television crews and curious observers hoping to catch a glimpse of the elusive "Lizard Man" said to have recently attacked a motorist as he changed a flat tire.

Meanwhile, Lee County Sheriff Liston Truesdale said others are calling to tell him they've seen the red-eyed creature, "and these are reputable people."

"We're running down a whole lot of rumors, but we'll cover what we can," Truesdale said.

Columbia radio station WCOS is offering a $1 million reward for the capture of the Lizard Man, which has caught the attention of monster hunters through the Midlands.

The State, Columbia, South Carolina,
July 23, 1988

Ring, ring.

Sheriff Truesdale picks up the receiver, then smiles a

smile that says this is—yep, you guessed it—another Lizard Man call....

The sheriff puts down the receiver and looks up.

"She's dead serious," he says.

The Charlotte Observer, Charlotte, North Carolina, August 14, 1988

Lizard Man is nationally known. A California "bigfoot" researcher has said the creature is a "skunk ape," more commonly known as bigfoot.

It debuted on "CBS Evening News" last week and will soon appear on PM Magazine. Lee County police say they get more than 200 calls a day about the creature, from as far away as New Zealand and Germany....

Belk advertising manager Sandy Jeffcott is convinced there's something big and green in the swamp—more than just money. "I'm not a disbeliever. Eventually, they're going to prove that something exists," she said.

The Charlotte Observer, Charlotte, North Carolina, August 16, 1988

"This is a very elusive sort of fellow that nobody can really put a handle on what it is, or where it came from, or what it really is all about," said Governor Carroll Campbell.